D0533079

THE GRUNTS
in a Jam

9112000024228

Praise for *The Grunts*

Philip Ardagh
THE GRUNTS
in a Jam

Illustrated by
Axel Scheffler

nosy
crow

*This book is dedicated to Wildlife SOS, fighting to save
India's wildlife, including the likes of Raju the elephant*

First published in the UK in 2014 by Nosy Crow Ltd
The Crow's Nest, 10a Lant Street
London, SE1 1QR, UK

HB edition first published in the UK in 2014 by Nosy Crow Ltd
PB edition first published in the UK in 2015 by Nosy Crow Ltd

Nosy Crow and associated logos are trademarks and/or registered
trademarks of Nosy Crow Ltd

Text © Philip Ardagh, 2014
Cover and inside illustrations © Axel Scheffler, 2014

The right of Philip Ardagh and Axel Scheffler to be identified as the author
and illustrator respectively has been asserted.

A CIP catal... available from the British Lib...ry

This book is ... of tra... or
otherwise, be ... circulated in any form ... g or
cover other tha... in which it is publishe... f this publication ...ay be
reproduced, store... a retrieval system, or transmitted in any form or by a... means
(electronic, ...chanical, photocopying, recording or otherwise) witho... he
prior written permission of Nosy Crow Ltd.

Printed and bound in the UK by Clays Ltd, St Ives Plc

Papers used by Nosy Crow are made from wood grown
in sustainable forests.

ISBN: 978 0 85763 075 9
ISBN: 978 0 85763 299 9

Check out the buzz at
www.meetthegrunts.com

CONTENTS

Chapter One
A Most
Tempting Nose

Mr Grunt was staring at a squirrel and the squirrel was staring back at Mr Grunt, with his big squirrelly eyes. (The squirrel had the squirrelly eyes. Not Mr Grunt.) The squirrel was a rather mangy-looking thing. His tail looked less like fur and more like a large feather that had been used as a quill pen and played with by small, sticky-fingered children. The animal was up a tree in a hedgerow lining a narrow lane. He stood on a swaying branch that seemed far too thin to take his weight.

1

Mr Grunt was leaning out of the upstairs bedroom window of the Grunts' truly dreadful caravan, his head framed either side by a curtain made from an old dressing gown. He was about the same height off the ground as the squirrel and – because the caravan almost took up the width of the lane – very close to the animal indeed.

It was obvious neither of them was going to blink and risk losing the staring match, so Mr Grunt decided to shout instead.

"Tree rat!" he yelled.

"Chrrrrrgggg!" chattered the squirrel.

"Clear off!" said Mr Grunt.

The squirrel quivered his tail in a don't-mess-with-me manner and ch-ch-chattered some more.

The problem, in Mr Grunt's eyes at least, was that he was convinced that this squirrel – this self-same squirrel, this *very* one – had been following them for days and was a THIEF. Whenever they stopped for a break, the squirrel would sneak among them and take some of Fingers' peanuts.

Fingers was the elephant who pulled the Grunts' caravan. This job used to belong to the two donkeys – Clip and her twin brother Clop – but they'd retired. They now had a trailer all of their very own, hooked to the back of the caravan, and Fingers pulled them all along with a wave of the trunk and the greatest of ease.

Fingers' favourite, favourite, *favourite* food was stale currant buns. I suspect an elephantologist at the University of Elephantology will tell you that it's far healthier for elephants to eat certain types of plant, but what Fingers liked best was BUNS.

He was also partial to peanuts in their shells – they made good snacks and rewards – so Mr Grunt took a regular supply from the local grocery store.

I say "local" because, unlike the old days where home was wherever they decided to park their caravan, the Grunts now had a base. They lived in the grounds of Bigg Manor, a stately home that looked very impressive from the outside but which was little more than an empty shell.

I say "took" because he – er – stole them.

The nearby grocery store was called Hall's Groceries and was owned and run by a woman called Miss Winterbottom. (The last Hall to work at Hall's Groceries was Mr Jon Hall, who died in 1887.)

Mr and Mrs Grunt used to laugh about Miss Winterbottom's name behind her back.

Actually, they also used to laugh about her name to her left, to her right and directly in front of her. And they *always* pointed.

One day, after about a year, Mrs Grunt came up with an extraordinarily clever and original nickname for Miss Winterbottom. She called her "Miss Cold Bum", laughed out loud at her own genius wordplay and then promptly almost choked on the dog biscuit she'd just popped in her mouth.

Having been called "Cold Bum" by other children since she was about three years old, Miss Winterbottom was neither impressed by Mrs Grunt's wit nor bothered by her name-calling. What she *was* bothered by was her shoplifting a dog biscuit, which is why she thwacked Mrs Grunt with one of those wide, flat-brushed brooms.

Mrs Grunt was a large woman, often

mistaken for a block of wood or an angry rock, so you could imagine *her* thwacking people with brooms, but Miss Winterbottom was a very different matter. She'd won the southern heat of the Miss Dainty Lady Shopkeeper Contest on a number of occasions. She was very petite, had golden hair and was generally thought to be very pretty indeed. Stick a broom in her hand, though, and it became a lethal weapon.

THWACK!

"Argh!" shouted Mrs Grunt, spitting masticated dog biscuit everywhere. "Stop it!" ("Masticated" is a grown-up word for "chewed", used by clever authors of children's books.)

But Miss Winterbottom didn't stop. "Stop..." she said. THWACK! "...hitting you..." THWACK! "...with this broom...?" THWACK! "Only..." THWACK! "...when you've paid..." THWACK! "...for that biscuit!" THWACK! She spoke with a beautiful sing-song voice, just loud enough to be heard above the THWACKS from the broom.

Sadly, what Miss Winterbottom didn't know was that Mrs Grunt was just a decoy (if now a rather battered and bruised one). Her job was to keep Miss Winterbottom distracted while the *real* thievery was happening at the back of her store. This was the first time Mr Grunt was making off with a large hessian sack marked "BEST PEANUTS".

What their almost-son Sunny told neither Mr nor Mrs Grunt was that, once he'd found out what they were playing at, he'd snuck back to the store after closing time and posted exactly the right amount of money to pay for the peanuts through the letterbox. He'd saved up the money from coins he'd found on the roads over the months, and earned from doing odd jobs for less odd people.

(NOTE TO ANY READERS WHO MAY NOT KNOW OR MAY HAVE FORGOTTEN: As a baby, Sunny had been either stolen or rescued by Mr Grunt, who'd found him hanging by his ears on a washing line. Cute or what?)

So the Grunts now regularly took – and Sunny regularly later paid for – sacks of peanuts from Hall's Groceries.

On more than one occasion, Sunny had wondered whether the Grunts secretly *knew* that he paid for the peanuts afterwards. On more than one occasion he'd found a surprising number of coins scattered along a single stretch of road. It was as though Mr Grunt might have gone ahead on that rusty old bike of his and tossed them there for him to find. But what would be the point of the Grunts nicking the nuts if they knew Sunny would pay for them straight afterwards? The excitement, perhaps? The thrill? The *naughtiness* of it all?

Whether the Grunts did or didn't know what Sunny was up to, it was some of these "BEST PEANUTS" from Hall's Groceries that Mr Grunt was *convinced* this staring-chattering-squirrel-up-a-tree was taking.

Mr Grunt leaned even further out of the bedroom window of the caravan. "THIEF!" he shouted (which was a bit rich, considering how he'd come by the nuts in the first place).

The squirrel studied Mr Grunt's nose.

Because Mr Grunt was angry, his nose was even redder than usual. It looked terribly bite-able. That was the word: *bite-able*. More than anything else in the world, that squirrel now wanted to bite Mr Grunt's nose.

He needed to.

He *had* to.

Nothing else would do.

Bite the nose! Bite the nose! Bite the nose!

With the rear-haunch wiggle of a lioness about to pounce on a passing gazelle, the squirrel launched himself at Mr Grunt, grabbed on to Mr Grunt's face with all four paws and sunk his teeth into the target...

...the *nose.*

UNG!

Mr Grunt screamed, grabbed hold of the squirrel and toppled forward out of the window, falling sideways from the caravan

with a

CRASH!
BANG!
THUD!
Arrgh!

With casual interest, Clip and Clop peered around the side of the caravan from their trailer hitched on to the back. They were both chewing slowly, and neither seemed surprised nor interested to see Mr Grunt – with a squirrel attached to his face – falling from the sky. They pulled their heads back in and got back to the important matter of eating, and of thinking donkey thoughts.

Fingers, hitched to the front of the van but stationary, turned his mighty head around, trunk high in the air, to see what all the fuss was about. He too didn't seem fazed by Mr Grunt rolling around in the narrow strip of lane between caravan and hedgerow, with a furry grey thing clamped to his face.

Mrs Grunt threw open a window at the side of the caravan and stuck her head out. "Keep the noise down, mister!" she yelled. "Some of us are trying to watch the goldfish."

The Grunts had an old television but it didn't have a screen. They'd replaced it with a fish tank, which they liked to sit and watch. They

found it soothing. Sunny liked them watching it too because it was one of the rare times of day when the pair weren't arguing with each other or with someone or something else (such as a squirrel).

It was Sunny who came to Mr Grunt's rescue. He'd been up front talking to Fingers, so had to push past the elephant's tree-trunk-like legs to reach him. He thrust his hand inside the pocket of his blue dress – he always wore Mrs Grunt's childhood dresses, dyed blue – pulled out a fistful of peanuts and threw them at his father and the squirrel.

Now, although the squirrel was enjoying biting Mr Grunt's nose, the truth was that it didn't match the *thought* – the delicious *anticipation* – of biting the nose. The lining-up of the nose in his sights had proved to be more exciting than the reality of the actual biting...

...and now he could smell peanuts. Lovely peanuts.

He let go of the raging Mr Grunt, snatched a peanut in his jaw and half-hopped, half-bounced (in the way that only squirrels can, however mangy) down the length of Mr Grunt before dashing up a different tree.

"Idiot!" said Mrs Grunt, possibly to Sunny or the squirrel but most likely to Mr Grunt, before slamming the window shut and padding back over to the sofa in her tatty bunny slippers, sitting herself down next to her cat-shaped doorstop and watching the goldfish again.

Sunny helped Mr Grunt to his feet. "Are you OK, Dad?" he asked.

"OK?" said Mr Grunt. "OK? Do I look OK?"

"Your face is a mess," Sunny admitted. "Does it hurt?" He pulled a clean hanky out of his dress pocket, causing the last few remaining peanuts to fall on the tarmac. Fingers' trunk came into view, sniffing, and delicately picked up a few of the nearest stray nuts. Sunny handed the hanky to Mr Grunt, who pressed it against his nose..

"The little vermin!" he said. "The... The..." He winced. Some of the squirrel bites seemed quite deep.

"I think we need to find a doctor, Dad," said Sunny. "You might need stitches."

"The nearest doctor could be miles away," said Mr Grunt, his voice muffled by the hanky – which was turning an impressive shade of red – in front of his face.

"There's one just here," said Mimi, appearing at Sunny's side. Mimi used to be Lord Bigg's boot boy at Bigg Manor (although she was a girl) but all that matters here is that she was Sunny's best friend and was with them on their journey.

"A doctor just where?" demanded Mr Grunt, through the hanky.

"Just up ahead," said Mimi, the two humming birds flitting around her head. Didn't I mention the humming birds? Sorry. They were called Frizzle and Twist (not that I could tell you which was which).

It was true. There was indeed a doctor's just up ahead. When Sunny had jumped down to see why Fingers had stopped in the lane – giving Mr Grunt the opportunity to have his altercation with the squirrel (who was now nibbling through the shell of his peanut) – Mimi had climbed out of the caravan and spotted a sign on a gatepost.

It read:

ALPHONSO
TUBB, MD
☆
DOCTOR TO
THE STARS

Mimi told Mr Grunt about it.

"He sounds expensive," said Mr Grunt.

"But not as expensive as losing your nose or bleeding to death or getting some horrible infection," said Sunny.

"Infection?" said Mr Grunt. "Your mother would *love* it if I got one of those. She'd laugh herself even more stupid!"

By "mother", Mr Grunt meant Mrs Grunt, not Sunny's birth mother. There was a time when Sunny had thought that he was the son of Agnes the cook and chambermaid, and Jack the Handyman (also known as Handyman Jack) from Bigg Manor, but that had proved not to be the case. He now knew there was the possibility that he was Horace, the missing son of the pig-loving Lady "La-La" Bigg and the bird-keeping Lord Bigg – whom they'd mislaid about the time Mr Grunt had found Sunny on the washing line – but he wasn't convinced.

And, despite the fact that Mr and Mrs Grunt spent most of their time calling each other names when they were together, it was obvious that Mr Grunt was *far* from happy at the thought of some infection keeping them apart.

So the decision was made. They would pay a visit to Dr Alphonso Tubb.

Chapter Two
A Way with Words

Dr Tubb was sitting at his writing desk in the bay window of his home, Green Lawns Villa, when – across the wide expanse of green lawns – he saw a caravan approaching: a hideous contraption made from everything from an old garden shed, parts of a motorbike-and-sidecar, an ice-cream van, some bobs from bits and bobs and just about anything else that Mr Grunt and his dad, Old Mr Grunt, could lay their hands on at the time. And, if that wasn't weird enough, it was being pulled by an elephant ... an elephant being led by what appeared to be a boy with the most sticking up of sticky-up hair, wearing a blue dress.

Back then, Dr Tubb would write postcards to Jenny Prendergast, a throat-specialist's daughter in the nearby town of Osprey, three times a day. Each postcard contained a new poem dedicated to Miss Prendergast that he made up as he went along (rather than getting it right on a piece of paper first before copying it out on to a postcard).

He had a photograph of his beloved Jenny, in a silver frame, on his desk in front of him, and would often glance up at it when writing. It was a slightly odd photo because it had originally been of Jenny with someone standing next to her, but Dr Tubb had cut out the other person, so there was a sort-of-person-shaped-space where the person had been. The doctor had cut out the other person for two reasons: firstly, because he wanted the picture just to be of Jenny; secondly, because the other person was none other than Norris Bootle. And Dr Tubb really didn't like Norris Bootle because he'd been Jenny Prendergast's childhood sweetheart. He was Alphonso Tubb's rival in love. (*Boo! Hiss!*)

When the Grunts rolled down his brick driveway, the lovesick Dr Tubb was on his second postcard of the day. Jenny Prendergast's address and the postage stamp went on the right-hand side of the card, so he had to cram his verse – written in his flowing hand – on to the left. He'd got as far as:

Oh Jenny, Jenny
Your virtues are many:
Your loveliness is vast
My favourite Prendergast
If you were a flower, I'd pick
you
If you were a ball I'd

when he was interrupted. He screwed the top back on to the end of his old-fashioned fountain pen with a sigh. It – the pen not the sigh – rolled off the desk and on to the thick-pile carpet with a silent, cushioned thud. (And yes, you CAN have silent thuds *because I say so*.) As he bent to pick it up, he reread the words he'd written so far. This was one of his best poems EVER, so he was more than a little annoyed to be interrupted part way through.

Moments later, the front door bell jangled. Dr Tubb reluctantly got to his feet and walked out of the carpeted drawing room and across the black-and-white marbled-tiled hallway. He opened the front door to be faced by the boy in a blue dress, a girl with pink-framed, pink-lensed glasses, pink bows in her hair and two humming birds flying above her head, and a lump of a man with a hanky over his face.

"Hello. Are you Alphonso Tubb, MD?" asked Sunny.

Dr Tubb nodded.

"Doctor to the stars?" asked Mimi.

Dr Tubb nodded. Again.

"My father has been bitten on the nose by a squirrel," Sunny explained.

Dr Tubb was already looking at Mr Grunt, who, quite apart from having a blood-soaked hanky covering most of his features, looked very odd. The doctor noticed, for example, that the man appeared to be holding his trousers up with a belt made from at least two smaller belts. His shoe laces obviously weren't really shoe laces. And then there was the smell.

"You'd better come in," he said, stepping aside. "Go straight through the door on your right." The last thing he wanted them to do was to go through the doorway on the left and have the man drip blood on his lovely, deep-pile, light-coloured carpet.

Sunny, Mimi and Mr Grunt went through the right-hand doorway to find themselves in a well-equipped doctor's surgery, with an examination couch, a screen to change behind, lots of gleaming gadgets and gizmos, an impressive desk and a wooden swivel chair with brass-studded green leather padding. The

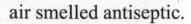

air smelled antiseptic.

Pulling the hanky away from his swollen and bloody nose, Mr Grunt looked around the room. "This room smells funny," he announced (which was a bit much coming from him).

Often when Mr Grunt was grumpy or upset, or just felt like kicking something, he'd – er – kick something. The something his foot came into contact with *this* time was a metal wastepaper bin. The bin clattered across the floor like a milk pail kicked across the milking parlour by a cow. It bounced and skittered, ending at Dr Tubb's feet. He bent down, picked it up and carried it over to Mr Grunt.

"Hold this," he said.

"Why should I?" demanded Mr Grunt.

"To catch the drips of blood," the doctor explained. "Now let's see what damage this

squirrel has done."

Dr Tubb studied Mr Grunt's nose quickly and efficiently.

"You're going to need stitches," he announced. "And a very big injection."

"A what?" demanded Mr Grunt.

"An injection," said Dr Tubb.

"Did you say a very *big* injection?" asked Mr Grunt.

"A very big one," nodded Dr Tubb.

The doctor got Sunny and Mimi to act as his assistants. Alphonso Tubb's nurse had Fridays off, so – it being a Friday – they had to stand in for her. Dr Tubbs soon realised that, despite his wonky-eared, sticky-up-haired, strangely dressed appearance, Sunny was a smart kid. And so was the sweet-smelling pink girl with the birds above her head. Once hands had been washed, it was down to business.

When it was all over, Mr Grunt's face had been cleaned and disinfected with something that left his skin looking yellow-tinged, highlighting the squirrel's claw marks. His nose was held together with six neat stitches, and there was a thick, padded dressing with sticking plaster over the top, holding it in place. Mr Grunt was also left with a sore bottom from that very large injection.

Dr Tubb peeled off his disposable latex gloves, opened the lid of the pedal bin with his foot on the pedal and dropped them in. He indicated Sunny and Mimi to do the same.

"Nice work, Sunny," he said. "You too, Mimi ... though I'm not sure they'd let you work in a hospital with those two flitting around." He pointed at Frizzle and Twist.

"Thanks, Dr Tubb," said Sunny and Mimi together.

"Now, I'm not going to hold my breath—" began the doctor.

"Then why tell us?" demanded Mr Grunt.

"I beg your pardon, Mr Grunt?" said the doctor.

"Why waste time telling us you're *not* going to do something? If we all stood around all day telling each other what we're not going to do, we'd never get ANYTHING done."

"Well—"

"Hey, doc! I'm not going to the moon."

"If you'd let me finish—"

"I'm not going to have a baby... Not even a baby grand piano!"

"What I was going—"

"Hey, doc! I'm not going to make shoes out of banana skins and slide from here to the North Pole!"

"– to say was that I—"

"Hey, doc! I'm not going to pay for this treatment because I don't have any money!"

"Precisely," said Dr Tubb.

"Huh?" said Mr Grunt.

"What I was going to say was…" He paused and cleared his throat. Mr Grunt remained silent. "I'm not going to hold my breath, but are you able to pay? I expect the answer to be no, but there's no harm in asking."

"Oh," said Mr Grunt. He looked quite endearing with his "nose bandage", if not exactly cute.

Just then, Sunny caught sight of something moving out of the corner of his eye. He looked over to the window just in time

to see the top of someone's head duck out of view.

Who's that, he wondered. *A gardener? Someone hoping to catch a glimpse of one of Dr Tubb's celebrity patients?* It certainly hadn't been Mrs Grunt. He'd recognise the top of her head anywhere. Curious...

"Dr Tubb is being *nice*, Mr Grunt," said Mimi, bringing Sunny's attention back into the room. "He just fixed up your nose and face and gave you an injection without asking whether we could afford it first."

Sunny turned to the doctor. "I'm sorry, Dr Tubb. But it was an emergency."

"No matter," said the doctor, eager to get back to his poem. The poems were, you see, extremely important to Dr Tubb. He saw them as the greatest weapon in his armoury to win the heart and hand of Miss Prendergast. And he need "weapons" because he wasn't the only man out there who wanted to make Jenny Prendergast his wife, remember. (There was his arch-rival, Jenny's childhood sweetheart Norris Bootle.) But Norris couldn't write poetry the way he could!

Back in the driveway, with Dr Alphonso Tubb closing the front door behind them, Sunny looked across to the window of the surgery where he'd caught sight of the person looking in. He was fairly sure that it'd been a man. There was no sign of anyone now, though there were plenty of shrubs and trees he could be hiding in. The three of them made their way back towards the caravan.

Mrs Grunt, meanwhile, hadn't wasted her time. She'd let Clip and Clop out of their trailer to have a feed. (They were busy enjoying the flowers in one of Dr Tubb's beautifully

tended flowerbeds.) And she'd also cut seven or eight neat strips of turf out of the lawn. She was busy rolling up the last of these and putting it into the back of the caravan, when her husband arrived.

"Let's get out of here," said Mr Grunt.

"Out of where?" demanded Mrs Grunt.

"I said *here*, didn't I?" said Mr Grunt.

"Where's here?" demanded Mrs Grunt.

"Here," said Mr Grunt, pointing at the ground beneath his feet.

"But I'm here," said Mrs Grunt, pointing at her patch of ground a metre or so away.

"Then let's get out of both of heres," said a triumphant Mr Grunt.

"Smart thinking, husband," said Mrs Grunt with a nod.

Sunny was busy herding Clip and Clop back into their trailer, the donkeys still happily chewing on ripped-up flowers. This was no way to repay Alphonso Tubb's act of kindness. But what could he do?

Soon the Grunts were trundling back down the brick driveway.

Back at his desk, Dr Tubb was yet to discover the damage done to one of the lawns of Green Lawns Villa and to a flowerbed. He was thinking of postcard poetry, and of the lovely Jenny Prendergast. He reread what he'd written on his latest postcard:

Oh Jenny, Jenny
Your virtues are many
Your loveliness is vast
My favourite Prendergast
If you were a flower, I'd pick you
If you were a ball I'd

Botheration! What with the unexpected interruption, he couldn't for the life of him remember what he'd intended to write next. He sighed, tore the card in half and tossed it

into the wastepaper basket.

He'd have to start all over again.

Just as the Grunts reached the top of the brick driveway, they were met by a woman driving a gleaming red motorbike and sidecar coming the other way. She screeched to a halt and lifted her goggles off her eyes. Instead of a normal crash helmet, she was wearing what looked like a Viking helmet with giant horns on it (not that Vikings really had horns on their helmets). In the sidecar was a boy wearing a similarly horned crash helmet.

"Holy fremolly!" said the woman, eyeing up the oncoming elephant and the caravan. "Those ears are big!"

The boy, who was probably about Sunny's age, gave a snort a bit like a friendly pig might. "Zoweeee!" he said.

"Sorry," said Sunny, who was sitting astride Fingers, Mimi just behind him. "Can you drive round us?"

"Not a problem," said the woman.

Sunny leaned forward and peered at her more closely from his high vantage point. "Er, excuse me," he said, "but aren't you Lara Farp, the famous opera singer?"

"She most certainly is!" said the boy in the sidecar proudly.

The woman smiled. "Indeed I am. And this," she said, nodding her head in the direction of her travelling companion, "is Ace."

Ace snorted again. The noise really reminded Mimi of Lady "La-La" Bigg's pig, Poppet.

"I'm Sunny," said Sunny.

"And I'm Mimi," said Mimi.

"Circus performers?" asked Lara Farp.

Sunny shook his head. He was used being

40

thought of as part of a circus. "No," he said.
"And we're not one of the stars treated by Dr
Tubb. Not like you, Miss Farp. He was just
kind enough to help us out in an accident."

"He's a lovely man," said Lara Farp. "Was that wet drip of a woman with him?"

"His nurse?" asked Sunny hesitantly. "No. Fridays are her day off, apparently."

"No, no, not her," said the opera singer, pulling the goggles back over her eyes. "I meant the doctor's love-of-his-life, Jenny Prendergast."

Ace snorted from the sidecar at the mention of her name.

Sunny shook his head. "No, Dr Tubb was alone."

"A lucky escape for you then!" said Lara Farp, who was clearly not a Jenny Prendergast fan. "Oh, well, must get on! Bye now!" She raised a leather-gauntleted hand in farewell, revved the bike's engine, then drove round them. Fingers raised his trunk and waved. Ace waved back from the sidecar, a big grin on his face.

"What's the hold-up?" shouted Mrs Grunt from inside the caravan.

"Lara Farp!" shouted Mimi.

"WHAT?"

"Lara Farp!" shouted Sunny.

"There's no need to be rude to your mother!" shouted Mr Grunt angrily, and Sunny heard him kick something.

"OUCH!"

That something was Mrs Grunt.

Chapter Three
Meet the Gloom Bag

Sometimes the Grunts took the caravan out on the open road to go in search of food. Most of their diet was roadkill – those poor squashed animals you often see run over by vehicles. (Mrs Grunt was, for example, very proud of her hedgehog goulash with crows' feet crispies.) They did, however, often send Sunny out on his own, on Mr Grunt's rusty old bike or just with Fingers.

Sometimes they took the caravan out simply because that was the life they were used to and they were feeling a bit cooped up in the grounds of Bigg Manor, which they shared with Lady "La-La" Bigg, her pig, Poppet, and a bunch of ex-servants, including Mimi (the ex-boot boy, remember?).

Sometimes the Grunts took the caravan out because they had places to go, and this journey was one such trip. They were on their way to collect Mrs Grunt's mother. Mrs Grunt called her mother "Ma" but her name was Mrs Lunge, rhyming with "sponge".

Mr Grunt wasn't too pleased about the trip because he really didn't like Mrs Lunge. He also suspected that she was one of those people who could be deaf when it suited them (in other words, not really deaf at all). And Mrs Lunge, in his opinion, was so depressingly gloomy about everyone and everything. In fact, Mr Grunt's nickname for Mrs Grunt's mother was Gloom Bag, said in an especially gloomy voice.

There had only been four people at Mr and Mrs Grunt's wedding, not counting Mr and Mrs Grunt themselves, or the man who married them. Everyone had a great time (even the policeman, to whom Mr Grunt was handcuffed at the time). Everyone, that is,

except for Ma Lunge.

"This church smells," she sighed. (They didn't get married in a church, it was a town hall.)

"It's cold in here." (She was hugging someone else's ice sculpture.)

"Everyone's mumbling." (No one was mumbling. She had suet in her ears.)

"Some idiot's blocking my view." (She was sitting behind a statue of the mayor.)

"This wedding cake is all leathery." (It wasn't a wedding cake, it was a handbag.)

"Your new husband has a face like a hippo's bottom." (She had a point there.)

Mrs Lunge also had a thing about not liking people taller than her. She took it as a personal insult and, being only 4ft 7in tall – that's about 1.397 metres – that meant that she didn't like most adults.

She also felt gloomy about the corns on her feet. "I never have enough!" she wailed.

She bemoaned the number of languages she could speak. "If only I couldn't speak any..."

She was depressed about her eyesight. "If it wasn't so good, I wouldn't have to see ugly people so clearly."

All in all, she felt that life was like one big card game and she'd been dealt a poor hand. Or it was an "everyone-gets-a-free-doughnut" party, and she'd been given the only one without any jam in it.

The one thing in Ma Lunge's life that regularly made her the slightest bit happy was her yappy little dog, Squat.

Squat was yapping now as, two hours after leaving the doctor's, Sunny pulled up the caravan alongside the tiny row of cottages where Mrs Lunge's house was to be found.

She lived in No 3, Railway Cottages. The windows were so grimy they were hard to see through, and there was an impressive layer of dead insects on the windowsills, inside and out.

Yap! Yap! Yap! went Squat.

Fingers looked at the little dog with his intelligent elephant's eyes.

Yap! Yap! Yap! went Squat, jumping up at him now.

Fingers patted her with his trunk.

Squat stopped yapping.

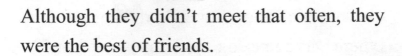

Although they didn't meet that often, they were the best of friends.

Ma Lunge shuffled out of No 3 in a pair of flip-flops so grimy that it was impossible to tell what their original colour might have been. Her toenails, however, were painted the brightest orange Sunny could remember having seen anywhere. Even on an orange.

"Oh," she sighed on seeing Sunny and the caravan. "You're here."

"Hello, Grandma!" said Sunny, trying to sound far more enthusiastic than he felt.

"Hello, Mrs Lunge," said Mimi.

Ma was eyeing Fingers. "I suppose that great grey hulk has been upsetting my poor little dog," she sighed.

"I think they're as friendly as ever," said Sunny.

"And what happened to the donkeys that used to pull this thing?" demanded Mrs Lunge. "They're dog food now, I suppose?"

"They're in their trailer at the back, as always," said Mr Grunt. He jerked his head in the direction of Clip and Clop.

"Where's Bunny?" asked Mrs Lunge. "Did she bother to come?"

"Of course Mum came," said Sunny, Bunny being Ma Lunge's name for her daughter, Mrs Grunt (who spent much of her life wearing bunny slippers).

"Mum!" Sunny called. "We're here and so's Grandma!"

Mrs Grunt opened the door of the caravan and stomped down the steps. She looked so BIG next to her tiny mother, standing in front of the tiny cottage. It was hard for Sunny to imagine them both living there, along with Mrs Grunt's dad before he'd been killed by a unicorn.

What do you mean, "there are no such things

as unicorns"?
Do you think
I'm as stupid as I
look? *Of course* there
are no such things as
living, breathing
unicorns. The
one that killed Mrs Grunt's dad was stuffed.
Well, it was a stuffed horse. Some Victorian
taxidermist – which is what professional
stuffers of animals are called – had added a
narwhal's tusk to the front of its head to make
it *look* like a unicorn, the sneaky old thing.
Anyway, that's what had killed Mr Lunge
years and years ago. It was being wheeled on
a trolley down the steep ramp at the back of a
delivery truck when … when… Let's just say
that it was a pointy, messy, tragic business.

"Hello, Ma," said Mrs Grunt. She leaned

forward and kissed her tiny mother on top of her head. "We brought you some lawn."

"Hello, Bunny," said Mrs Lunge. "What would I want with lawn?"

"Well, we don't want it," said Mrs Grunt.

Mrs Lunge sighed.

The mention of lawns – well, the turf stolen from Green Lawns Villa – made Sunny find himself thinking of the person at the window again. The man had already been ducking from view as Sunny'd turned to look. If only he'd got a look at his face and not just a quick glimpse of the top part of his head.

What was he up to? he wondered.

When Sunny had mentioned the man to Mimi earlier, she'd thought it was most likely he was a fan hoping for an autograph from a star, or a journalist or photographer hoping for a news story or a photo.

"And instead he got Dad with a squirrel bite on his nose!" said Sunny.

"And an elephant pulling a caravan!" Mimi laughed.

Speaking of the caravan, of all the new arrivals at No 3, Railway Cottages, Mrs Lunge was most pleased to see Clip and Clop. Despite what she'd said about dog food, she loved those donkeys and went over to their trailer and fussed over them.

"What happened to you?" she asked Mr Grunt as she passed him. She reached up – a long, long way for her – and jabbed his bandaged nose with a bony finger.

"OUCH!" said Mr Grunt. "A good-for-nothing squirrel," he said.

"A good-for-stuffing what?" said Mrs Lunge, patting Clip – or was it Clop? – on the muzzle.

"I didn't say anything about stuffing!" said Mr Grunt. "I said, '*good-for-nothing*'. A good-for-nothing squirrel."

Mrs Lunge turned and GLARED at him.

"What did you just call me?" she demanded.

Mr Grunt sighed. "I'll be inside if anyone wants me," he announced, clambering back into the caravan.

Squat was now jumping up and barking at Frizzle and Twist, who were treating the whole thing as a game. They were swooping up and down, tantalisingly just out of the little dog's reach.

Sunny handed Mrs Lunge a carrot to feed to the donkeys. She took it, snapping it in two and giving each donkey a piece. They chewed it thoughtfully and appreciatively.

"Staying long, Bunny?" she asked Mrs Grunt.

"You know we're just here for the night, Ma—" Mrs Grunt began.

"Then why come?" demanded Ma Lunge. "You're not here to steal my rare plate

56

collection, are you? I knew it! You ARE, aren't you?"

In truth, Mrs Lunge only owned two – very ordinary – plates but she loved them. She had even named them. The chipped blue one was called Blue Plate, and the unchipped (but slightly cracked) red one she called Red Plate. Mrs Grunt's mother scrabbled up the wooden steps to the caravan to get nearer to her daughter's height, then GLARED at her.

Mrs Grunt sighed. The only person she found more annoying than her beloved Mr Grunt was her mother. "No, Ma. We're not after your plates. We're here to take you to the country fair nice and early in the morning, remember?"

"Course I remember," said Ma Lunge, who'd completely forgotten. "What do you take me for?"

"An idiot!" shouted Mr Grunt from inside the caravan.

The walls did little to muffle the sound of his guffaws but Mrs Grunt's tiny mother seemed not to hear a thing. "This year I'm going to beat that Edna Tuppenny fair and square!" she said.

"Or, failing that, we can cheat," muttered Mrs Grunt. Edna Tuppenny was her mother's arch-rival in the all-important annual

Preserves, Jams and Jellies Competition at the fair. She was the thorn in her mother's side.

"As long as you don't expect me to sleep in that thing overnight," sighed Mrs Lunge, eying the caravan suspiciously. "It might fall apart and kill me in my sleep."

"Course not, Ma," said Mrs Grunt. "You sleep in your own bed tonight. We don't want you waking up dead, now, do we?"

There was another loud guffaw from inside the caravan.

Chapter Four

Pants

Bright and early the next morning, Jenny Prendergast read the latest poem from Alphonso Tubb for a third time:

Jenny Jenny you're the best
You're like my favourite Sunday
    vest.
I long to be with you forever more.
But unlike the vest just
    mentioned,
I wouldn't keep you in a drawer.

She sighed. No one wrote poetry like her beloved Tubby. If only she were clever like him: doing all that doctory stuff that doctors do AND being such a brilliant poet.

She picked up the photograph of him in the heart-shaped frame and kissed it on the already lipstick-covered glass. She'd decorated the frame herself with seashells and pieces of broken glass from one of Alphonso's empty medicine bottles. Some of the bits of glass still had a reddish tint from where she'd cut her fingers gluing them down. Broken glass can be like that sometimes. Then she picked up the photograph right next to it. This was in a plain silver frame and was of a smartly dressed young man with a smile that showed off his two rows of perfect white teeth.

"Oh, Norris," she sighed. "I love you too."

And she kissed the glass of that photo as well.
But then she thought once more of Alphonso's
poetry. Oh, the *poetry*!

Her thoughts were interrupted by none other
than the very Norris Bootle I just mentioned
popping his head around the door.

"Knock knock!" he said, instead of

knocking. "Hello, Jenny, old girl!" he said. (She was three days older than him.)

"Norris!" said Jenny with a sickening squeal of delight. Then she remembered that she was supposed to be annoyed with him about something – she usually was – so she frowned. "What are you doing here?" she demanded.

"I thought you said you wanted me to drive you to the country fair with all your silly old jars for the Preserves, Jams and Jellies Competition?"

She looked at Norris. He always seemed to be wearing the same checked suit nowadays. Once upon a time it had been rather snazzy, but that once upon a time had been long, long ago.

"What's that?" asked Norris, looking beyond Jenny to the piece of paper lying on the table.

"Nothing!" said Jenny, quickly snatching up the poem but Norris simply snatched it off her in turn. "That's private!" she squealed. "Don't you dare read it!"

But childhood sweetheart Norris Bootle *did* dare read it, much in the same way that, back in their school days, he'd snatch privately-passed-around-notes off her.

"This is piffle!" he said with a snort.

"What-le?"

"Piffle," said Norris.

Jenny Prendergast had no idea what piffle was but she could tell by the way that Norris said it that it was NOT a good thing.

"You're beastly!" she said, throwing herself on a sofa so covered in cushions that it looked more cushion than sofa. She pummelled a few with tight fists, for good measure. "Beastly, beastly, beastly."

"Come on, old thing," said Norris, suddenly looking sheepish. He thrust the poem back into her hand. "I was only joking. It's not the worst poem I've ever read."

"It isn't?" said Jenny between sniffs, not that she'd been crying.

"No," said Norris. "Not by a long way." He was thinking of some of Alphonso Tubb's poems he'd read on the postcards pinned up in his Jenny's bedroom when he'd gone looking for a pair of scissors one time. He was particularly fond of the dreadful opening lines:

Jenny with the face so pretty
Lovely lips and nose not drippy.

He'd been wandering around eating a dainty cake when he'd first read it. (Norris was a man who liked to eat on the move.) He'd done such a big snort of laughter that a couple of almond flakes – which were decorating the top of the cake – had shot right up his nose. (But it wasn't a *piggy* snort, unlike the kind Ace made.)

Jenny got up from the sofa and rearranged her dress, smoothing it down at the front. She then studied her face in a small, round wall-

mirror, patting her hair into position. She smiled, liking what she saw. Jenny was, in fact, what many people thought of as pretty. It was only when she said or did anything that most people wanted to run away, feeling a little sick.

"Now, where are your preserves, jams and jellies? We do need to get them in the car," said Norris.

Jenny Prendergast didn't like Norris's car, which was, in fact, a small van. It came with his job. Because that job was selling underwear for The Hearty Underwear Company, it had the words THE HEARTY UNDERWEAR COMPANY written on both sides. Because The Hearty Underwear Company sold underwear for men AND women, it had a picture of a pair of frilly, spotted women's knickers below the writing on one side, and a pair of equally spotted but not-at-all frilly men's pants on the other.

Jenny had been very glad when Norris had got a job but was embarrassed by what that job was. She could never imagine herself being married to a man in underwear (if you see what I mean). She'd looked forward to the day he got a different, better job. But he

hadn't. It seemed that he *liked* the idea of being a Hearty Underwear man for life. But even more embarrassing than the job was being driven around in a vehicle with big pictures of pants on it, something which didn't seem to bother Norris in the slightest.

Soon they were both in the van, he behind the wheel and she with the carefully jarred and neatly labelled preserves, jams and jellies – her competition entries – on a wooden tray on her lap.

Breakfast at Mrs Lunge's that morning was really a variety of different breakfasts. Clip and Clop each had a nosebag of oats. Fingers had some currant buns. Mimi had some fruit (a bit bruised), while Mr and Mrs Grunt and Sunny had some home-made muesli – which, along with some of the donkeys' oats, included wood-shavings and sheep's dandruff – with fox's milk. In her own little kitchen, Ma Lunge had bacon and eggs on Blue Plate and a slice of very ordinary, very nice toast on Red Plate.

When she'd washed up, she went out of No 3, Railway Cottages, up the steps of her daughter's caravan and knocked at the door, Squat yapping at her feet.

Sunny opened the door. "Morning, Grandma!" he said. "All set for the country fair?"

"I'll get my things," she sighed. She stomped back down the steps, across the pavement, through the garden gate and up the short path. "Come on!" she called. "Follow me!"

A few minutes later, Sunny emerged from the house carrying a large cardboard box. Although the words "BONZO'S DOG

TREATS For the Discerning Dog" were printed on the side, this is not what was in the box. The cardboard box was full of the jars of Mrs Lunge's home-made preserves, jams and jellies that she would be entering into the competition at the fair.

The top of each jar was covered in a piece of red-and-white checked cloth, held in place with an elastic band. Each jar was also clearly labelled in Mrs Lunge's surprisingly neat handwriting.

Squat, who'd just been having a quick staring contest with Clip and Clop, bounded excitedly over to Sunny and began jumping up at him, yapping. Sunny found it difficult to carry a box full of jars while a dog seemed to be doing her very best to trip him up.

Ma Lunge swooped down – it wasn't that far – and picked up Squat in her arms. *Yap! Yap! Yap!* went the dog, and then licked her mistress's face with her long, pink tongue. "Well, what are we waiting for?" said Ma Lunge.

Sunny was suddenly blinded – briefly – by a flash of light.

"Argh!" he said, shielding his eyes. "What was that?"

"Are you OK?" asked Mimi. "The flash came from over there." She pointed to a fenced-off area of scrubby trees and bushes running along the side of the railway track, on the opposite side of the street. "It must have been sunlight reflecting off glass or something – look!"

Someone tall, thin and *pointy* was trying to slink off unnoticed between the shrubs. Despite the sunny weather, they were wearing a long coat and a baseball cap.

Mimi and Sunny could clearly see a pair of binoculars in their hand. The sun's rays must have reflected off the lenses into Sunny's face. *Is this person the one who was peering through Dr Tubb's window?* Sunny wondered. And, if so, did this mean that it was *he*, Sunny, who they were interested in?

Sunny would have liked to have known the answer to *that*.

Chapter Five

To the Fair

Traditionally, the judge of the Preserves, Jams and Jellies Competition at the country fair was Lord Bigg of Bigg Manor but, unfortunately for him, he was currently in prison. The new judge was none other than Lord Bigg's wife, Lady "La-La" Bigg.

Lady "La-La" Bigg hadn't actually lived with Lord Bigg for a long time before he went to prison. While he stayed in the big, empty house with Monty his parrot, she'd lived in a rather nice pigsty in the grounds. A VERY nice pigsty, in fact. And she shared it with her very best friend in the whole-wide-world who went by the name of Poppet the pig.

Lady Bigg was one of the few people who actually seemed to like the Grunts. Maybe *like* is a bit of an exaggeration. She certainly liked Sunny, but she was also perfectly happy to have Mr and Mrs Grunt live on her property. So when, later that morning, the Grunts' caravan came rolling into the country fair ground, Lady Bigg was one of the few people not to scatter. While others snatched up their children, cried, "It's them!" or, in one case, dived for cover inside a large sawdust-filled barrel used as a lucky dip, her ladyship simply waved at them with a cheerful "CooooEEEE!"

As for Poppet the pig, she'd fallen in love with Fingers the very first time she'd laid her little piggy eyes on him, the very last day

Lord Bigg spent at Bigg Manor. Poppet had somehow got it into her piggy heart and mind that the elephant was a very large pig – and an extremely handsome one at that.

Mr Grunt stopped the caravan in a taped-off area of grass, knocking over a traffic cone marked "NO PARKING" in the process. Usually he'd have Sunny up at the front riding Fingers, but he'd wanted to get away from Mrs Grunt's mother, who'd been complaining from the moment they'd set off.

"This caravan is full of melons," she'd moaned.

"*Melons are good for you.*"

"Your television is stuck on one channel."

"*It's a goldfish tank.*"

"It's very cold in here."

"*You're leaning out of the window.*"

"That cat keeps staring at me."

"It's not a cat. It's a doorstop."

The cat-shaped doorstop in question used to be called Ginger Biscuit because it looked like a ginger cat ... until, one day, Mr Grunt had absent-mindedly used it as a paintbrush when he was repainting Clip and Clop's trailer.

When he'd realised his mistake, he'd been genuinely upset – because he knew just how much the cat-shaped doorstop meant to Mrs Grunt and she (secretly) meant a great deal to him – so he'd done his best to wash the paint out. The end result was that Ginger Biscuit still looked like a cat but not a ginger one. Mr Grunt had been dreading what Mrs Grunt would say when she saw it, or what she might do. To him.

What had actually happened, though, was that she'd walked in, picked up the now muddy-brown cat-shaped doorstop, said,

"Hello, Chocolate Biscuit!" and wandered off with it as though he'd always looked like that and had always had that name.

"It smells of old lawns in here," Mrs Grunt's mother had said, glaring at the few remaining pieces of turf cut from Dr Tubb's garden.

That'd been the last straw. Mr Grunt had gone up front and taken charge of Fingers, and Sunny had gone inside to talk to Mimi. Not surprisingly, their main topic of conversation was the person at the surgery window and the one over the road outside Mrs Lunge's house.

"Do you think they were the same person?" asked Mimi.

"Couldn't say," admitted Sunny. "I'm as certain as I can be that the person outside Dr Tubb's window was a man, but I don't know if the one with the binoculars was a man or a woman."

"It's weird enough one person spying on you, but *two*!" said Mimi. "What on earth's going on?"

They'd now reached the car park and Mr Grunt had knocked over a cone or two. A man clutching a book of raffle tickets was jumping up and down and shouting furiously, "You can't park your contraption here! Didn't you read the signs?!"

"No," said Mr Grunt. "I didn't." One of the Grunts' favourite pastimes was *not* bothering to read signs.

The furious man stomped right up to the Grunts' caravan. He was about to get VERY bossy with Mr Grunt, which would no doubt have made Mr Grunt VERY angry when – fortunately for everyone else at the country fair – Poppet put in an unexpected appearance.

Lots of kicking was avoided.

The pig came barrelling towards the caravan, more like a very excited, very overweight dog than a piggy. She was making the happiest of squealing noises. She'd spotted Fingers and

was DELIGHTED. Here was her biggest and best piggy friend in the whole wide world (except, of course, for the fact that he was actually an elephant).

In an effort to avoid the hurtling pig, the raffle-ticket man leaped backwards directly into the path of a small flock of passing sheep. They were being led from the back of a large, wooden-slatted trailer to the country fair's holding pens, which were off to one side of the car park, and he very quickly found himself having to do some very serious apologising to an annoyed-looking farmer.

Poppet, meanwhile, was swooning at the sight of handsome Fingers, who was patting her on the back with his trunk, as he had Squat the dog. Mr Grunt jumped down on to the grass, which was still damp with morning dew, and Mrs Grunt and her mother spilled out of the back of the caravan. Mrs Lunge was clutching an enormous misshapen handbag.

"This is going to be the worst country fair ever," she announced before she'd even reached the bottom step. She looked up at the clear blue sky. "I don't much like the look of the weather either."

"There isn't a cloud in sight, Ma," sighed Mrs Grunt.

"Precisely," said her mother. "There could be a drought! We could all die of thirst."

"Not in a *day*, surely, Grandma?" said Sunny, appearing in the doorway behind her. He was carrying the big cardboard box marked "BONZO'S DOG TREATS For the Discerning Dog", full of the jars of Mrs Lunge's home-made preserves, jams and jellies. "We'd better enter these into the competition."

"Insects!" said Mrs Lunge.

"Insects?" said Mrs Grunt.

"Insects?" said Mimi, who'd come out behind Sunny. She looked around for any gnats or flies or wasps or – Heaven forbid! – bees. "I don't see any insects."

"Exactly," said Mrs Lunge. "Not enough water, and the insects die of thirst. Not enough insects to feed on, and the birds die of hunger. Not enough birds, and—" She paused to brush a fly off her nose.

"See, Ma?" snorted Mrs Grunt, glaring at her tiny mother. "More than enough insects to go round."

Mrs Lunge looked disappointed. "Have you seen the dry, parched earth?" she demanded, tucking her huge handbag under one arm and pointing.

Sunny looked down at the lovely, lush, dewy green grass of the field being used as the country fair car park. "No, Grandma," he said.

"Exactly!" said Mrs Lunge. "They've obviously been wasting precious water keeping it this way! Babies in their cots and prams, with cracked lips and dry tongues, gasping for water and—"

"Are you *still* complaining?" muttered Mr Grunt, stomping by.

"WHAT did you just say?" demanded Mrs Grunt's mother. "Did you say something about raining? We're in the middle of a DROUGHT here and you're making jokes about rain?!"

"There isn't a drought, Grandma," said Sunny soothingly. "We were just discussing the weather, remember?"

Mrs Grunt, meanwhile, was staring at Mr Grunt. There was something different about him.

A new hole in his old sweater?

No.

Fresh plasters on his squirrel wounds?

No, not that either.

He'd cleaned his shoes?

Definitely not.

He was wearing a traffic cone on his head?
Ah, yes. That was it...

"Why've you got that cone on your head, mister?" she shouted.

"It was the nearest cone I could find," said Mr Grunt.

"I meant, why are you wearing it on your head?"

"Then say what you mean."

"Then answer the question."

"I've forgotten the question."

"Why ... are ... you ... wearing ... a ... traffic ... cone ... on ... your ... head, you leg-warmer?"

"Because it won't fit on me knees, you shaving brush!" snapped Mr Grunt.

"Cushion cover!"

"Hash browns!"

"Horse hair!"

"Privet hedge!"

"Privet hedge?" gasped Mrs Grunt.

"Privet hedge," nodded Mr Grunt.

"You... You..." spluttered Mrs Grunt. "You bone marrow!"

Sunny plonked the cardboard box on the grass, causing the jars inside to chink. The others stopped and looked.

"Careful with those, Sunny," said Mrs Grunt.

"Sometimes I don't know why I bother entering," muttered Mrs Lunge. "The whole competition is fixed, rigged, a con..."

"But you won once, Ma," Mrs Grunt reminded her.

Her mother didn't seem to know what to say to that, so changed the subject. "Where's Squat?" she asked.

This was a good question because there wasn't the annoying yapping that usually accompanied Squat when she was around.

"Don't let anyone step on this or, worse still, park on it," said Sunny, pointing at the box of preserves, jams and jellies on the ground. He turned and went back inside the caravan to look for his grandmother's tiny dog.

Squat was sticking out from under the upturned hubcap that Mrs Grunt used as a bowl, and Sunny had a sudden flashback to

the time when Mr Grunt had been hiding under their upturned tin bath until Mrs Grunt had managed to force him out and get under it instead. I'm sure I have a picture of her hiding under it somewhere…

Oh, here we are. You may even recognise it from *The Grunts All at Sea*.

Sunny scooped up Squat in his arms, causing the dog to start her usual yapping. Somehow she also managed to lick Sunny's face between yaps, which he half liked – it was loving and it tickled – and he half-didn't, what with all that yucky slobber.

"Ah, there you are, my gorgeous thing,"

said Mrs Lunge to her dog, in that voice of hers she only used when talking to animals.

But Squat was more interested in Fingers than she was in her mistress. To be more precise she was interested in the way Poppet and Fingers were behaving together. She looked from the pig to the elephant and back again, shook as though she were shaking water off her fur, then started up her yapping *again*.

"I think Squat's *jealous*!" said Mimi with a laugh.

"Of what?" asked Mr Grunt.

"Of Poppet and Fingers!" said Mimi.

"That pig does get soppy around Fingers, it's true enough," said Mr Grunt. "And if that yap-dog has taken a shine to old big-ears—"

"I do NOT have big ears," interrupted Mrs Grunt's mum, hitting Mr Grunt in the stomach with her huge handbag. (The handbag was big by anyone's standards but, being such a tiny lady, in Mrs Lunge's hands it looked enormous.)

"Oooooff!" said Mr Grunt, doubling over, clearly winded. The traffic cone fell from his head, bouncing to the ground, narrowly missing the cardboard box. You would have

said exactly the same if you'd been hit in the tummy with that handbag, and you probably didn't even know that "Oooooff!" was a word.* [*EDITOR'S NOTE: It isn't.]

"Dad didn't mean *you*, Grandma," said Sunny. "He was talking about Fingers."

"Funny how your mother can hear perfectly well when it suits her!" said Mr Grunt to Mrs Grunt between gulps of air.

"I heard that!" said Mrs Lunge.

"That's just my point!" said Mr Grunt. (And it was a good point.) Mr Grunt was standing upright now but looked a little pained. He stood well back from his mother-in-law in case she took another shot with that bag of hers.

"Enough of this idle chattering!" said Mrs Lunge. "Let's get my jars over to the competition marquee… Where is it, exactly?

I expect they're trying to hide it from me."

"Follow me!" said Sunny, who had little idea where the marquee was but was beginning to fear that they might spend all day at the bottom of the steps to the caravan. He picked up the big cardboard box marked "BONZO'S DOG TREATS For the Discerning Dog". "This way!"

Mrs Lunge followed hot on his heels, as fast as her little legs could carry her, her bright-orange toenails glinting in the morning light. She was looking from left to right, eyes darting here, there and everywhere. She was on the lookout for Edna Tuppenny, the woman who might ruin her chances of becoming Preserves, Jams and Jellies Competition Champion yet again.

"But not this year," she muttered. "No, not this year."

Chapter Six
New Friends

Norris Bootle brought his van to a halt in the lane leading to the car park of the country fair. He pulled over to one side, parking half up on a grass verge and half on the tarmac. His now-grown-up childhood sweetheart, Jenny Prendergast, had INSISTED that he didn't park in the field that was being used as the car park because it would be too, *too* embarrassing to arrive at the country fair in a van with pictures of pants on the side.

"Come on!" said Jenny Prendergast, already

striding down the lane towards the entrance, holding her wooden tray of jars of preserves, jams and jellies out in front of her.

"Hang on, old girl!" called Norris, quickly locking The Hearty Underwear Company van.

Just then a shiny red motorbike and sidecar appeared around the corner of the lane, taking the bend rather sharply, causing the wheels of the sidecar to lift off the ground for a moment.

"*Way-hay!*" shouted Lara Farp, her operatic voice projecting clearly above the noise of the engine.

"Coooooooooooool!" shouted Ace from beneath his horned helmet in the sidecar.

They swerved to avoid Jenny Prendergast – causing her to rattle her jars in surprise – each recognising the other in that instant. Lara Farp didn't like Jenny because she, like Ace, thought the woman was a "wet drip" and

"an insult to womanhood". Jenny Prendergast didn't like Miss Farp much because she thought famous people, such as the opera singer, should behave with more dignity in public and not like some loud "wanna-have-fun" person all the time. And she certainly didn't like Miss Farp's snorty boy, Ace.

"Sorry!" shouted Lara Farp as she took a

sharp right-hand turn into the field being used as the car park. She didn't particularly sound as if she meant it.

Norris caught up with Jenny. "Isn't that Lara what's-her-name?" he said excitedly.

"Farp," said Jenny. "Yes. She's one of Alphonso's patients."

"Well, he *is* a doctor to the stars," said Norris, quoting the line on the notice outside Dr Tubb's house in a childish sing-song voice.

"At least he has a proper job," said Jenny Prendergast. "*He* doesn't sell underwear."

"You didn't think there was anything wrong with my selling underwear before Tubby came along, now, did you?" said Norris, which was half true. As I've said before, Jenny had always wished her childhood sweetheart had sold anything other than underwear, but was pleased that he'd got the job *because it meant that he could buy her nice things.* "By the way, do you know where Miss Farp buys *her* underwear?" he added.

Jenny Prendergast gave Norris a look. "Why are you asking *me*?" she demanded.

"I thought lover-boy Tubby might have mentioned it in conversation," said Norris.

Jenny glared at him. "And why should Alphonso know where Lara Farp buys her undies, I'd like to know?" she said.

Norris thought about that. "Well, patients do tell their doctors the most personal things," he said.

Jenny Prendergast thrust the tray of preserves, jams and jellies into her childhood-sweetheart's hands. "You carry these for a while. And do be careful," she insisted. "They're ever so precious to me ... just like Alphonso." She fluttered her eyelids in a way a butterfly might flutter its wings just before it crash-lands.

"You used to sigh and flutter your eyelids when you talked about ME," said Norris, feeling all sorry for himself. He kicked a stone.

"I did," agreed Jenny, "but that was when I was young and foolish and before I met Alphonso." She sighed again, probably to annoy him. No, that's not true. It was *definitely* to annoy him.

"I was just wondering whether I could get Miss Farp to wear Hearty Underwear," said Norris. "What a coup that would be: World Famous Opera Singer Wears The Hearty

Underwear Range!"

Jenny Prendergast stopped in her tracks. Norris stopped too.

"What is it?" he asked.

"This is MY day," she pouted. "We're at the country fair because I'm entering a competition – not you – and you're not going to spoil *everything* by trying to sell people underwear." Her lower lip quivered and her saucer-like eyes glistened. It looked to Norris as though she might be about to burst into tears; something she did no more than ten or eleven times a day.

"No, Jenny. Of course not," he said. "I wouldn't dream of it."

But Norris did have a surprise in store. He loved Jenny too and wasn't about to give her up that easily.

Sunny found the marquee where the Preserves, Jams and Jellies Competition was to take place. It wasn't hard. There were plenty of signs dotted around the country fair to point him in the right direction. Sometimes Mimi would run ahead, spot a sign and report back. (She also spotted a number of signs about A SPECIAL GUEST APPEARANCE FROM WORLD-FAMOUS OPERA SINGER, LARA FARP.)

Sunny, Mimi, and Mrs Grunt's mother peered through the entrance of the marquee. The Preserves, Jams and Jellies Competition was just one of the competitions that were being judged in the huge tent, each with entries laid out on white-tablecloth-covered tables stretching into the distance.

"Wow!" said Sunny.

A woman, wearing blue-rimmed glasses

and clutching a clipboard, was standing by the entrance to the marquee. She studied the pink girl with the tiny birds hovering above her head. She eyed the boy with the wonky ears, wearing a blue dress and carrying a big cardboard box marked "BONZO'S DOG TREATS For the Discerning Dog". Mrs Lunge was up on tiptoe, resting her chin on his shoulder.

"Entrant?" asked the woman, because only those entering the competition were allowed in before midday.

"Of course he's not an elephant!" said Mrs Lunge with a sigh. "We left the elephant back at the caravan. He's a BOY."

"Entrant," the woman repeated with a sigh. "Competition entrant?"

Mrs Lunge eyed the woman suspiciously. "I suppose you're going to disqualify me before I even have a chance to get through the tent door, aren't you?" she sighed. "I suppose you're going to tell me that I have to be taller than I am to enter... I'm too small, aren't I? That's it, isn't it? I'm too small." She turned around. "Come on, you two. Let's go."

"Yes, we're competition entrants," said Sunny to the woman, before Mrs Lunge had a chance to say anything else.

"For the Preserves, Jams and Jellies Competition," Mimi explained.

"Name?" asked the woman, lifting the pages clipped to her clipboard until she found the right one for the competition.

"Lunge," said Sunny, and then he spelled it.

The woman found the name on the list and ticked it off. "Very well," she said, and then directed them where to go to lay out their jars.

Once Sunny and Mimi had unloaded the jars from the cardboard box on to the tabletop, he pushed the empty box under the table where it was hidden by the overhanging tablecloth. Then they left Mrs Lunge to sort out her display of jars. Had it been Mr or Mrs Grunt, Sunny wouldn't have dared leave them alone but he was pretty sure Mrs Lunge would be able to cope without ruining everything for everyone. So he and Mimi went to see what else was happening at the country fair.

They saw some familiar faces as they explored, including – much to Sunny's surprise – a clown called Mr Lippy, whom he hadn't seen in a long time. Mr Lippy was dressed in full clown clobber: lime-green giant shoes, comedy trousers with funny stretch braces, checked jacket with a squirty flower in the lapel, clown wig, red nose and full clown make-up. He was sitting on an upturned bucket changing the front tyre of his tiny clown-bike.

Mr Lippy recognised Sunny in an instant. (Looking and dressing like Sunny made him difficult to forget.) "Hello, Sunny!" he said. "How's Fingers?"

"Very well, thanks, Mr Lippy," said Sunny, thinking back to the time he and Mr Lippy had first met (which I wrote about in *The Grunts in Trouble*). "He's in the car park with Mum and Dad."

"I might go and say hello later on," said the clown, "once I've repaired this puncture and done a bit of entertaining."

A moment later, Sunny bumped into Ace. Literally.

"Ooof!" went both boys – though not necessarily with the same number of "o"s –

and both fell to the grassy ground.

"Hey, sorry, man!" said Ace, getting to his feet first, grabbing Sunny's arm and yanking him up too. "Couldn't see where I was going." He undid the chinstrap and lifted the horned crash helmet off his head, tucking it under his arm. "This thing kind of keeps slipping over my eyes." He adjusted a small hearing aid hooked behind his left ear.

"I like your Viking horns," said Sunny (though, as I said earlier and I'll say here for the last time – in this book, at least – Vikings never really had horns on their helmets like that).

Ace smiled. "Lara's in this opera where she wears a horned helmet, so she thought it'd be cool to have a couple of crash helmets made like this for us to wear. His 'n' Hers."

"Is she your mum?" asked Sunny.

Ace shrugged. He had a lot of straw-like hair. "She didn't give birth to me if that's what you mean," he said. "But she's my mum in everything but name. She once said that even if she were my birth mum she'd never want me to call her 'Mum' because that isn't how she does things... What's with the dress?"

Sunny looked down at his clothes. He never really thought about them. He had an elephant and two donkeys to look after, as well as coping with life with Mr and Mrs Grunt. His dress was just one of those things.

Now *he* shrugged. "Dunno, really," he said. "It's just what my mum gives me to wear. What's that thing behind your ear?"

"It's a hearing aid," said Ace. "I'm kind of deaf without it. Hi, Mimi." He remembered their names from their brief encounter in Dr Tubb's driveway the previous day.

"Hi, Ace," said Mimi, strolling up beside them.

"Cool hummingbirds," said Ace. "And I like your elephant, by the way."

The three of them chatted as they wandered around the country fair.

During this conversation it turned out that the biggest thing the two boys had in common was that neither Sunny nor Ace knew who their birth parents were.

"Your dad – Mr Grunt – rescued you from a washing line?" gasped Ace when Sunny told him.

"That's what I said," Sunny nodded.

"Pegged up there by my ears."

Ace looked at Sunny's ears, one much, much higher than the other. "Is that why they're –?"

"Maybe." Sunny shrugged.

"And you never found out *whose* washing line?"

"We live in a caravan," Sunny explained. "We were always on the move back then. I don't think Dad would have been able to find the washing line if he wanted to."

"Don't you remember anything about your parents?" asked Ace.

They were passing a clearing between the tents where a blacksmith was showing a small crowd of people how he made horseshoes. He was hammering a red-hot piece of metal into shape on the edge of an anvil.

"All I can remember is a pair of very shiny men's shoes and a woman with a beautiful voice. I think the shoes might have belonged to my dad and the voice might have belonged to my mum... I thought I'd found them a while back: Agnes the ex-cook-and-maid and Jack the ex-handyman up at Bigg Manor where we now live."

"You live in a manor house?" said Ace.

"The remains of one," said Mimi.

"It's falling to bits," said Sunny, "and, unlike Mimi, I mostly live in the caravan in the grounds."

"But they turned out not to be your parents?"

"No," said Sunny. He decided not to mention that he was now considering the possibility that he was actually the missing child of Lord and Lady Bigg because he didn't really have any evidence to go on. "What about you?"

The blacksmith gave the hot horseshoe two final CLANGS with his hammer, then – using a huge pair of metal tongs – plunged it into a barrel full of cold water that bubbled and steamed with a loud HISSSSSSSSSSSSS as the metal cooled.

"Me?" said Ace. "The way Lara tells it, she found me left by the stage door of the opera house in Pring, in a wicker shopping basket, which is pretty cool." Pring was a nearby town. "Her fans are always leaving her presents and stuff, so she guessed I must be one. She's always been too busy to find time to have a kid of her own, so she decided to keep me."

"Do you remember anything about *your* birth parents?" asked Sunny.

"It'll sound silly..." said Ace.

"Wearing a Viking crash helmet is silly!" Mimi laughed.

"It's just that in my mind..." Ace faltered.

"What?" asked Sunny.

"Well, in my mind I have a clear image of my father and..."

"And?"

"And I think he was a pirate captain," said Ace.

Chapter Seven

A Whole Lot of DON'Ts

Mr Grunt was quick to make his presence felt at the fair. It began when he sat on the guess-the-weight-of-the-cake cake, protesting, "What does it matter that it's flat? It still weighs the same!" as he ran away from the furious stallholder. (He was rather overlooking the point that the prize for guessing closest to the weight of the cake *was the cake itself* ... and who in their right mind would want a flat cake with an imprint of Mr Grunt's bottom on it?)

Next, he knocked over a stack of locally-

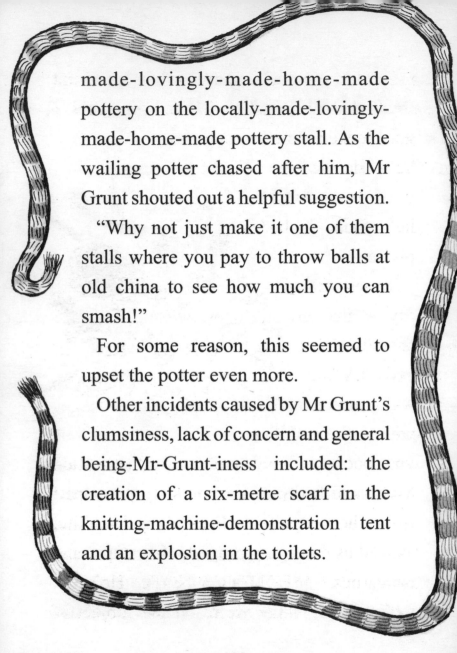

made-lovingly-made-home-made pottery on the locally-made-lovingly-made-home-made pottery stall. As the wailing potter chased after him, Mr Grunt shouted out a helpful suggestion.

"Why not just make it one of them stalls where you pay to throw balls at old china to see how much you can smash!"

For some reason, this seemed to upset the potter even more.

Other incidents caused by Mr Grunt's clumsiness, lack of concern and general being-Mr-Grunt-iness included: the creation of a six-metre scarf in the knitting-machine-demonstration tent and an explosion in the toilets.

The last one had occurred when Mr Grunt found the only available loo had somehow got blocked with fir cones, and he'd decided to clear it with a firework he'd found in his pocket.

It goes without saying that you should never, ever, EVER walk around with a firework in your pocket or anywhere else for that matter. You could badly injure yourself, quite apart from other people, pets, livestock and wildlife, as well as damaging property. It's stupid and dangerous.* [*EDITOR'S NOTE: He's not joking.] But, while we're on the subject of don'ts, I could add:

DON'T sit on a guess-the-weight-of-the-cake cake.

DON'T smash locally-made pottery.

DON'T tamper with the settings on other people's knitting machines.

DON'T blow up toilets, whether it's with fireworks, a stick of dynamite or plastic explosives.

Is that clear? I do hope so. I wish it had been for Mr Grunt. If, from the start, all the different people he'd upset had realised that Mr Grunt had been responsible for all those *other* people's upset, dotted about the field, then he'd probably have been chased away from the country fair, or arrested much sooner. As it was, to begin with most victims thought they were the only ones who'd had the misfortune to have a visit from Mr Grunt.

Mr Grunt, Mrs Lunge, Sunny, Mimi and Ace eventually came across each other. Sunny, Mimi and Ace were eating toffee apples on sticks. Mrs Lunge was pacing around, staring at her orange-toenailed feet, and fretting about the Preserves, Jams and Jellies Competition and how she was *bound* to lose because Edna Tuppenny was *bound* to have cheated somehow or bribed the judges. Mr Grunt was busy picking off bits of cake from his clothing (popping each piece in his mouth, of course). They met, by chance, by a big round tent made of animal skins. Such tents arc called yurts. Mr Grunt had been in a yurt just once before and had found it very dark and very *smelly*.

"Hello, waste-of-space," said Mrs Lunge to Mr Grunt.

Mr Grunt wasn't sure how to respond to

that so he kicked the nearest thing: the wall of the yurt.

There was a THUD from inside.

This was followed by a GROAN.

This, in turn, was followed by an "Ayyyyyyyyeeeee!" and a little girl – with her face half-painted like a beautiful blue butterfly, but with a thick, jagged line running across her nose and cheek – came screaming out of the tent. She was followed moments later by the face-painter who Mr Grunt must have kicked over as she sat the other side of the yurt wall. Shaken, the face-painter still clutched her paintbrush in her hand.

Next, the little girl's father appeared. He looked angry. No, more than angry. He looked *outraged*. He was trembling with rage. He looked around to see who had caused his precious daughter – his little *princess* –

such upset. His eyes fell on Mr Grunt. The two men locked stares.

Mr Grunt pointed at Sunny. The dad turned his attention to the boy.

A second later, Sunny was running for what seemed like his life, with the furious dad in hot pursuit.

Mrs Lunge looked at Mr Grunt. "What did you do that for?" she demanded.

"What did I do *what* for?"

"Why did you point at Sunny? Why did you make old beetroot face think it was him who'd kicked the tent, not you?"

"That's a *why* not a *what*," said Mr Grunt with immense satisfaction. (Wasn't such witty wordplay proof of what a clever chap he was?)

"*Why* then, idiot-chops?" said Mrs Lunge.

"Sunny can run much faster than me," said Mr Grunt.

Mrs Lunge considered the answer, tilting her head to one side and then the other. "You have a point," she said. Perhaps her son-in-law wasn't quite so stupid after all.

As for Mimi and Ace, they were chasing after the dad chasing after poor old Sunny, on the run for a kick he hadn't even committed.

Sunny darted this way and that: around

tents, through tents, over prize goats, between the legs of a woman on stilts – her performing name was Tall Tanya Lee, in case you were wondering – and over a barrier into another field.

Sunny risked another quick look over his shoulder to see that, for the first time, the dad (who'd started out bright red with rage and now was unbelievably redder still from all the running) had lost sight of him for a moment and was looking in the wrong direction.

Sunny had to act fast. He needed to hide and he needed to hide NOW.

Without a second to waste, he clambered into the nearest hiding place.

Guess where that hiding place was.

Oh, go on. Don't be a spoilsport. Guess.

Not in a tree, no.

He hid in the front cockpit of one of two biplanes parked side by side in the field.

What do you mean, *why I didn't mention them before*? They weren't important before. They were just two biplanes, one red and one blue, parked side by side in an otherwise pretty much empty field. (Biplanes are those old-fashioned types of plane that have two wings either side, one above the other, held together with struts and supports, and have open-air cockpits with no roofs.)

And Sunny was now hunched up in a ball

in the front cockpit – there were two – of the blue plane, and pulling himself as low down and out of sight as possible. He could hear someone coming and hardly dared to breathe. The plane rocked a little as someone climbed into the other cockpit.

Mimi and Ace were as baffled as the angry dad, who'd given up and was now stomping off in search of his partially face-painted princess. Where on *earth* had Sunny gone?

Only, technically, now Sunny wasn't on the earth… The blue biplane had just taxied down the field and taken to the skies.

Today was an important day for Alphonso Tubb, MD, doctor to the stars, but – although it involved the country fair and his beloved Jenny Prendergast – it had nothing to do with Jams, Jellies and Preserves, for it was Dr Tubb who was in the other cockpit of the blue biplane, piloting the controls.

This was no ordinary biplane – if biplanes can be considered ordinary – because this particular biplane was also a skywriting plane: a plane used to write messages in the sky with its vapour trail. And now Alphonso was ready for action! He checked his watch. Jenny would have had to have finished laying out her preserves, jams and jellies by now, in time for the judging, which meant that she would be enjoying herself at the fair.

All he had to do was to wait for the next

meticulously timed moment of his plan. His heart beat with excitement; that self-same heart that was filled with love for dearest Jenny. (Yes, I know. This is all a bit sickening, isn't it?) There was a loudspeaker system set up around the fair, with outdoor speakers rigged up on special stands. It was mainly used for announcements, such as when the next prizes would be awarded, or when the locally-made-lovingly-made-home-made-pottery stall hoped to reopen, or reuniting a bright-red dad with his daughter with a zigzag-painted face. But suddenly, right on cue, music started playing from the speakers.

Music always sounds terrible – tinny and thin – coming through this kind of speaker but this music sounded even worse than usual. Firstly, because it was played on Dr Tubb's battery-operated keyboard, which didn't sound great at the best of times. Secondly, because the doctor had recorded his playing and singing – yes, I did indeed say singing – on the machine that he usually dictated his doctor's notes into. It wasn't designed for music. Thirdly, because Dr Alphonso Tubb had not only been making up the tune as he recorded it, but he'd also written the song's lyrics himself.

Remember his poems?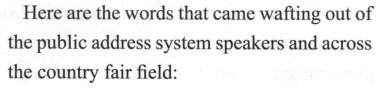

You do?

Then you see the problem.

Here are the words that came wafting out of the public address system speakers and across the country fair field:

Jenny Prendergast,
Lift up your pretty eyes,
Cos up in the sky's
A nice surprise!

Then came the part when he would start

writing the actual message with the vapour trail. This was the part he'd been practising in secret for months.

Up in the skies
Is a plane that is yellow,
And the person who is flying it
Is that man-who-loves-you fellow.

Unfortunately, as you may recall, the plane was in fact blue but Alphonso had no idea what colour the plane would be when he wrote the song and he chose yellow because he could think of something that it would rhyme with. He wasn't that bothered that the plane turned out *not* to be yellow because of "artistic licence" – where an artist can change the facts to suit his art, as in *tell a lie* – and the fact that it was unlikely there'd be another plane up above the country fair at the same time. And so the song continued:

And the message he's writing
Is meant just for you!
Be sure to say "Yes!"
Doo-bee doo-bee doo!

and yes, you're right, the *Doo-bee doo-bee doo!* part was particularly dreadful.

So the music had started playing and it had the desired effect. Hearing her name, Jenny dashed away from the stroke-the-fluffy-bunnies stall to see what was going on, closely followed by Norris Bootle.

When she saw the plane she squealed in delight. "That's Tubby up there!" she chirped. (Along with Sunny, of course, but she didn't know that then.) "My Tubby!"

Now crowds of people were gathering in clusters, looking up to see what was happening. People spilled out of tents and away from stalls.

The plane began to write:

Just then, *another* biplane came into view. It was the red one that had been parked next to the blue one in the field. This one was piloted by a chap called WingCo Fish. (WingCo isn't a name but is short for Wing Commander.) He too was on a mission remarkably similar to Dr

Tubb's but on behalf of a certain Mr N Bootle from The Hearty Underwear Company. He did quite a lot of work for Hearty's (which is what had given Norris his brilliant idea).

WingCo Fish had a message to deliver but, unlike with Dr Alphonso Tubb's biplane, this message wasn't written out in a live-as-it-happened vapour trail but on a long, thin banner pulled behind it.

The banner that Norris had supplied the pilot with was supposed to read:

JENNY PRENDERGAST BE MY
GIRL FOREVER NORRIS XXX

but somehow there had been a mix-up. The banner that was now unfurled behind the plane and stretched out like a fluttering ribbon was the one WingCo Fish often used for the company. It read:

BE A SMARTY MAKE YOUR UNDERWEAR HEARTY

There was laughter from the crowd.

There was a gasp of horror from Norris Bootle.

Jenny Prendergast looked from the banner up in the sky down to Norris Bootle at her side. Then back up again. She burst into tears, running into the nearest tent to hide her upset and her shame.

Chapter Eight

Disaster Strikes!

Now, I'm rather hoping that at least *some* of you are wondering how poor Sunny was doing while all this was going on. You're probably well aware how important it is to wear a seatbelt in a car, so imagine how important it was for him to be wearing a seatbelt in an open cockpit of a biplane being flown by a part-time pilot. And not just flown but whooped and swooped and loop-the-looped as Dr Tubb formed the letters of his skywriting message.

When Alphonso Tubb first spotted Sunny

in the cockpit in front of his, as the boy nervously raised his head from hiding, he let out a surprised, "What the devil?" but Sunny heard none of it. The doctor's words were snatched by the wind and whisked away behind him, rather than in the direction of Sunny's ears.

When Sunny turned and looked at him and gawped, clinging on to the rim of the cockpit until his knuckles were white, Dr Tubb recognised those ears at once. "Sunny Grunt!" he gasped in amazement.

Under just about any other circumstance, Dr Tubb would probably have turned the plane round and gone in to land immediately, but he was at the start of a meticulously planned mission where timing was everything and he may never have the opportunity again. And anyway, if the boy had stowed away for a bit of adventure, where was the harm in that? Sunny had seemed a sensible boy back at the surgery and was bound to have strapped himself in good and tight.

What Dr Tubb didn't know, of course, was that Sunny had had no idea the plane was about to take off. To him, it had just been a hiding place. Strapping himself in had been the last thing on his mind.

Sunny was in for a bumpy ride.

With most people on the ground distracted by the aeroplanes up in the air, Mrs Grunt decided that now was a good time to make sure that her dear little mum – Mrs Lunge to you – beat the dreaded Edna Tuppenny in the Preserves, Jams and Jellies Competition. Of course, the only way she could make sure that her mother's food tasted better than her arch-rival's was by making sure that Edna Tuppenny's entries tasted truly dreadful. But how could she do that?

Simple! Sabotage (which is a great word for "deliberately destroy, obstruct or damage"). Hmmm. Well, Mrs Grunt certainly didn't plan to *destroy* Edna's preserves, jams and jellies – it would be a bit of a giveaway if Edna's jars were smouldering shards of exploded glass – but she might *obstruct* their chance of winning by causing some *damage* though!

Mrs Grunt had come out of the caravan to see what all the music, "Ooooh"-ing and "Aaaaah"-ing, and aeroplane-engine noises were about, and decided that now would be the perfect time to strike. She clambered back up the caravan steps in her bunny slippers.

Once inside, she flipped up the cushion of the very sofa where she'd been napping not ten minutes previously (clutching her favourite cat-shaped doorstop, Chocolate Biscuit). Space was hard to come by in the caravan, so any extra storage room was very useful indeed. The sofa was where Mrs Grunt kept, among other things, what she called her Rummage Bag (a cloth bag full of odds and ends). Tossing aside a half-rotten melon, she pulled out the bag and thrust her hand inside it. There was a terrible snapping noise and she yelped.

She pulled out her hand to find her fingers stuck in a mousetrap. Stuck to the other side of the trap was a note. It read:

in Mr Grunt's handwriting. Mrs Grunt chuckled at the cleverness of her husband while at the same time planning her revenge!

She freed her hand from the mousetrap and stuffed it back in her Rummage Bag, this time de-snapped and harmless. She slipped the strap of the bag over her shoulder and was ready to go.

Little did she know that she'd been watched all this time by someone crouching outside the caravan, peering through a window, the top of their head hidden beneath a baseball cap. Now that Mrs Grunt set off in search of the Competition Marquee, the coat-wearing figure followed at a distance.

When Mrs Grunt reached the tents, just about everyone was outside watching the planes. Looking left and then right, she got down on to the grass on all fours, pulled up a section of canvas wall at the side of the Competition Marquee, then crawled inside it on her hands and knees.

There was no one else in sight. She looked along the rows of tables and spotted the jars of preserves, jams and jellies on three long tables about halfway down, between the tables of Most Overweight Pumpkins and an Under-

12s competition for Vegetables Looking or Smelling Most Like Famous People.

Mrs Grunt didn't want to add something to Edna Tuppenny's jars that would make Lady Bigg unwell when judging. She just needed to add some *nasties*.

Mrs Grunt rummaged in her Rummage Bag. It was FULL of those.

At first, she considered adding a dash of *Blow's Extra Strong Chilli Sauce*, say, or some dried, crushed wild garlic, but she decided that this might be a bit of a giveaway. So what to choose? Whatever she chose, she didn't have much time. She set to work.

It was all going fine until the second biplane – the red one, flown by WingCo Fish, pulling the Hearty Underwear banner – flew on to the scene and Jenny Prendergast ran sobbing into the nearest tent...

Unfortunately for Mrs Grunt, the nearest tent was the very Competition Marquee where she was, and the tear-soaked Miss Prendergast burst in just as she was adding a dead fly to a jar of Edna's jelly.

Their eyes met.

Jenny Prendergast screamed just as Norris Bootle appeared behind her.

"No one but the judges is currently permitted in—" said a voice, which turned out to belong to the lady with the blue glasses, clutching a clipboard, who was spilling in after them. She too saw Mrs Grunt. "Madam," she said. "Explain yourself!"

"She was tampering with the jars!" said Norris. "I saw her! She was *tampering*!" (If truth be told, he was grateful for something – anything – to distract Jenny from the unfortunate Hearty-Underwear-banner-mix-

144

up-based interruption to Dr Alphonso Tubb's skywriting. If only his banner had carried the "Be Mine Forever" message he'd planned, how different things might have been.)

"You're ... you're CHEATING!" wailed Jenny Prendergast, with the kind of horror the rest of us would reserve for discovering someone eating an endangered species in a sandwich.

"Am not!" said Mrs Grunt.

"Are!" rasped a voice that sounded as if it belonged to a lizard that ate gravel for a living.

Everyone turned to look at who'd spoken: a newcomer to the tent, a tall, angular woman with sharp features and very flat hair.

She was sweating. It was Edna Tuppenny. "I've had my eye on your mother and you!"

"I am not cheating," said Mrs Grunt, which was technically true. She *had* been cheating but had *stopped* when they'd all piled into the marquee.

"Then what precisely *are* you doing?" demanded the lady with the clipboard.

"She was trying to help me find my contact lens," said a voice that made everyone jump. Moments later, Ma Lunge appeared from under the table. "I was looking on the ground here while she was checking my jars to see if it had fallen in one of them," she said, brushing a few blades of grass off her knees. "But the lens is bound to be lost or trodden on," she sighed. "Or both."

"Right," said Mrs Grunt. "So true." She might have been more convincing if she

146

hadn't so obviously been as startled as the rest of them.

"Contact lens?" said the clipboard lady. "A likely story. I'm going to have to ask you to come with me!"

Mrs Lunge was on her feet now. She fixed her eyes on those of her arch-rival. "Oh, there you are, Edna," she sighed. "I was wondering when you'd show up and spoil the party."

Edna Tuppenny was about to reply when she was interrupted by a few loud bangs followed by an enormous explosion.

To explain the KABOOM – because that's what the explosion sounded like – we need to go back just a little bit, to when Dr Alphonso Tubb's so-called music first started wailing out of the speakers and people looked up to the sky. While all this was going on, Mimi, Ace and Mr Grunt were part of only a handful of visitors to the country fair who'd not stopped doing what they were doing to see what all the fuss was about up-in-the-air.

Mimi and Ace were still looking for Sunny.

"He can't have vanished into thin air," said Mimi, as Frizzle and Twist flitted above her head. "And he must know that angry man's not still after him after all this time."

"I'm running out of places to look," said Ace.

Just then, something came hurtling out of the sky and landed on the tea tent to their left. It skittered down the tarpaulin roof and landed at Mimi's feet with a crunch. She looked down at it. It was a toffee apple, just like the ones she, Ace and Sunny had been clutching when the red-faced dad was in hot pursuit. Just like the toffee apples being eaten by men, women and children all over the fair...

...but how come this one had *fallen out of the sky*? Now Mimi looked up at the biplanes: the red one with a pilot and the blue one with a pilot and a passenger. She could clearly see someone in the front cockpit waving his arms about.

No! Surely not, she thought. *It can't be ... can it?*

But what was Mr Grunt up to? I hear you ask. Well, I don't actually hear you ask – probably because you're not asking or, if you are, you're much too far away – but I'll tell

149

you anyway. Mr Grunt was busy looking at the GUESS THE NUMBER OF BEES IN THE HIVE display. The local beekeepers' association had brought along a special hive. The sides were made of the usual overlapping pieces of wood, painted white, but the usual roof – which doubled as a lid – had been replaced with a glass one. This was so that people could look inside and see the busy, buzzy bees at work.

The prize for the person guessing the closest to the beekeeper's own estimate of the number of bees would win a very large jar of honey. Mr Grunt wasn't particularly interested in honey – though he had enjoyed pouring some into a pair of Mrs Grunt's shoes one time as a little surprise, and it certainly improved the taste of some of the roadkill – but he loved the jar. Though made of glass, as jars often are, this one was shaped like a huge trophy, with a base, a stem, a handle on either side and a lid with a knobble on top. It looked like a see-through football-championship-cup. Once the honey was used up, he could rinse it out and use it to show off the marbles and special glass eyes (shaped like complete eyeballs) he'd collected over the years. It would be perfect!

"How much a guess?" he asked the woman staffing the stall, dressed in her full beekeeping clothing, including a round hat with a veil to protect her face.

The woman eyed him nervously through the veil. She'd never actually met Mr Grunt before but she'd heard talk of him, and the plaster-over-the-nose made him seem even more – er – what's the word? Odd.

She told him the price.

Mr Grunt grunted, pulling a small woman's purse from his trouser pocket. I don't mean "a small woman's-purse" in that the purse was small. I mean "a small-woman's purse" in that the purse belonged to a small woman: Mrs Lunge. Mr Grunt had decided to look after her purse for her without wasting time by asking her first.

He pulled out a clump of coins and shoved them into the beekeeper's gloved hands, without checking the amount. "I want six guesses," he said. Then he leaned over the top of the hive, pressing his nose right up

against the glass roof, peering deep inside. "It's impossible to tell how many there are in there!" he grumbled, his breath misting the glass. "S'not fair."

"Everyone has an equal chance of estimating," said the beekeeper.

"Well, I wants a *proper* look," said Mr Grunt and – before she could say "Don't be a fool!" – he'd prised off the glass roof with his fingers.

"Wait—" began the woman, reaching forward to try to get the lid from him.

This annoyed Mr Grunt so much that he kicked the hive.

Now, to accompany the sound of the skywriting and Hearty Underwear planes up in the air, there was a loud buzzing of bees down on the ground: a swarm of bees that were even MORE angry and annoyed than

153

Mr Grunt was ... and they were chasing him.

Mr Grunt ran around stalls like a metal ball in a pinball machine, the bees in stingingly hot pursuit. He *zoooooooooooomed* past Mr Lippy, who was now juggling for an audience of one – a boy of about five or six – because the rest of the crowd had drifted off to look up at Alphonso Tubb in his plane.

The boy had stayed watching, mesmerised, because Mr Lippy was now juggling flaming clubs.

It was one of these clubs that Mr Grunt snatched from the stunned clown as he ran past, the bees close behind. Mr Grunt had once been told that bees didn't like smoke, so waving around a flaming club seemed like an excellent idea.

He waved it this way. He waved it that. He waved it in a figure of eight. He even tried a figure of nine. Basically, he waved that flaming club all over the place, without ever slowing down from an all-out run. The bees were just seconds behind him.

Waving the club certainly wouldn't have been a *bad* idea, if he hadn't dashed through a gap in a fence leading to a separate field, where the end-of-day fireworks display had been set up (the opposite side of the fair to the field which the planes used as a grassy runway).

Tripping over one of the ropes fencing off an area in the centre of the display, the torch flew from his hands into a cluster of firework rockets.

As the bees finally reached Mr Grunt, the flames of Mr Lippy's torch lit the blue touchpaper – the fuses – and the rockets burst into life…

Unfortunately, among the fireworks was a prototype for a brand-spanking-new firework rocket that wasn't yet officially on the market. It was called the OOMPH 5.

Most fireworks go up in the air so far and then no further. The prototype OOMPH 5 rocket went up 200 metres without pausing for breath, and then climbed higher and higher still...

And the end result? KABOOM!

(Yes, *that* KABOOM! The one on page 147.)

Chapter Nine
Come on Down!

Funnily enough, Sunny was not unfamiliar with planes unexpectedly hurtling downwards. I was going to say "hurtling to the ground", but the last hurtling plane he'd seen – well, if truth be told, the *only* one he'd seen – had hurtled into the sea not to the ground. And, anyway, the big difference between that occasion and this was that, in this instance, he was *inside* the plane.

At least he was now strapped in. When he'd almost fallen out earlier – when Dr Tubb was banking the plane to write one of the letters, and his toffee apple had gone spiralling into the sky below – he'd grabbed the belt and managed to lash himself to his seat. He had his eyes tight shut, partly out of fear and partly to try to keep the gushing wind out of them. Alphonso Tubb and WingCo Fish weren't wearing their fancy flying goggles just to look good.

And why was the blue biplane hurtling downwards?

Alphonso had just finished skywriting the line and had been in the process of framing the whole message in a heart. Meanwhile, WingCo Fish had been losing altitude – aeroplane talk for losing height – in the Hearty Underwear plane as he prepared to land.

This meant that, when most of the firework rockets shot up into the air and exploded with a shower of colours, they were a long way from either plane. But, when the massive OOMPH 5 firework kept on going, it was WingCo Fish's Hearty Underwear plane that it hit.

The OOMPH 5 was big, packed with gunpowder and, by pure fluke and/or misfortune, it hit the plane's propeller. The damage was done. Not only that, some of the sparks from the rocket even sprayed into the open cockpit, setting fire to the pilot's trousers.

WingCo Fish said some extremely rude words and started trying to beat out the burning embers on his trousers with one hand, while trying to control the plane spiralling out of control with the other. This wasn't his best day in the air.

High above, Dr Tubb spotted the red plane in trouble far below. His natural instinct as a doctor and an amateur pilot was to help and – without pausing and without warning – he put the old biplane into a nosedive, to try to reach the stricken red plane. Sunny could do nothing but hold on tight and hope for the best. And – oh yes – go, "Aaaaaarrrrrrgggggghhhhhh!!!"

Alphonso Tubb didn't actually own the blue

biplane. He was a doctor to the stars and one such patient was the film star Dirk Norwich. Dirk had put the doctor in touch with stuntman Zac "Buckwheat" Harris, who had his own skywriting plane, and had spent the previous few weekends teaching Dr Tubb how to fly it.

As the doctor took the biplane down almost vertically – and Sunny felt as though his stomach had somehow ended up in his not-so-level ears – two things happened: the engine made a strange coughing sound, and a rather important lever came off in Dr Tubb's hand, followed by a stream of cogs and nuts and bolts trailing up in the air behind it.

"*That's* never happened to me before!" he wailed, not that Sunny could hear him up ahead, which was also directly below, remember. They were heading DOWN.

Sunny had one thought on his mind at that moment: *We're going to die! We're going to die! We're going to die!* and I suspect that if anyone were to ask him, "Can you imagine things getting worse?" he would – between screams – have shouted, "No!" or shook his head.

But they did get worse.

Their plane had now caught up with WingCo Fish's plane, and the propeller became entangled in the HEARTY UNDERWEAR banner.

This was not good news.

Back on the ground, Mimi was acting fast. Following the falling toffee apple and familiar arm-waving, she was convinced that Sunny was in that plane. She'd hurried to the caravan with Ace and, hearing the "KABOOM!", dashed over to Fingers the elephant.

"Quick, Fingers!" she said. "Up!"

The elephant eyed Mimi for a moment with his intelligent elephant's eyes then carefully wrapped his trunk around her waist, lifted her up and gently plonked her down on his back.

"You coming?!" she called down to Ace.

"Where?" asked Ace.

"To reach the planes when they land," said Sunny.

"Crash, more like," said Ace. "You bet!" Fingers lifted him up and placed him behind Mimi, with Frizzle and Twist just above her head.

"Come on, Fingers!" said Mimi. "I think Sunny is up there. Follow those planes!" She gave Fingers a handful of the peanuts she'd grabbed from his nearby sack. The elephant took them in his trunk and popped them in his mouth as he lumbered off through the car park.

With WingCo Fish's biplane struck by the OOMPH 5 and propeller-less, and Dr Tubb's and Sunny's plane hurtling downwards, Mimi and Ace wanted to get there FAST. Which is why, when they reached the first hedge, Mimi didn't spend too much time looking for a gap or a gate but simply said, "Straight through, Fingers!" and urged the elephant on.

Fingers didn't need telling twice. He trampled through the hedge and was in the next field, gathering speed.

"Hold on tight!" shouted Mimi, talking to

Ace this time.

"What do you think I'm doing?" shouted Ace. This was turning out to be a very exciting day indeed.

✳

Dr Alphonso Tubb had never been so frightened in all his life, and he'd been through some pretty frightening moments over the years. There was the time Bing Bong, the famous magician, turned up at his surgery and sawed him in half, and an instance when he ended up hanging from the window ledge up on the forty-fourth storey of a hotel when he mistook the window for a door. But nothing compared to now, being strapped in a crippled biplane swooping down at crazy speeds.

The doctor came to the conclusion that the best way to fight the fear was to make the most of the situation, so he threw back his head and let out a "Yahooooooooh!" It was the sort of "Yahooooooooh!" a cowboy might make before facing a horde of attacking American Indians all on his lonesome.

It would have been loud enough for Sunny to hear up front if he hadn't been howling in panic too. Meanwhile, down below, Mimi and Ace charged through the fields on Fingers' back, trying to keep sight of the two stricken biplanes in the sky just up ahead of them, and Norris Bootle had reached his Hearty Underwear van.

"Come on, old girl!" Norris called out to Jenny Prendergast, who was hurrying down the lane behind him. There was an unspoken truce between the two of them. First, they'd have to find her beloved Tubby and see if he was all right, THEN she could blame him for the TOTAL EMBARRASSMENT of the

BE A SMARTY MAKE YOUR UNDERWEAR HEARTY

banner.

By the time Jenny reached the passenger door, Norris was inside the van and firing up the engine. She jumped in and barely had time to close the door behind her before he had pulled out into the lane. There was a screech of tyres on tarmac as he sped in the general direction of the planes.

Thanks to Fingers, with his wide elephant

strides, and their travelling directly across the fields, Mimi and Ace were the first to reach WingCo Fish's plane. They arrived just as it skimmed the top of a clump of trees, the stubby remains of the banner fluttering from the tail fin like a fish out of water in the throes of life. (All that was left was:

 The

part had been ripped off, spun around and caught up in the other plane's propeller, right in front of Sunny's terrified eyes.)

With amazing skill, WingCo Fish skimmed his plane across the top of the trees and actually managed to land it on its wheels. The little red biplane bounced off the ground then down again, then up down, up down, up down, before finally nose-diving into the ground.

But there was no mighty bang.

No burst of flame.

Back on the ground, the wing commander had freed himself and had run from the cockpit as fast as he could, towards Mimi and the others.

Moments later, the bottom of Alphonso and Sunny's biplane clipped the top of the self-same set of trees, ripping the two front wheels from the aircraft. They were left stuck in the branches, like two cherries on stalks, while the plane hurtled on.

Struggling with what was left of the controls, the doctor attempted to land the old biplane – front-wheel-less – in the far corner of the field where the red plane now rested. The field was full of sheep. The bleating animals scattered

in all directions and then, because sheep generally like to follow OTHER sheep, darted in yet more directions in the hope of finding other sheep to follow...

Thanks to Dr Alphonso Tubb's surprisingly impressive piloting skills, the plane actually hit the ground straight enough for it skid along the grass on its undercarriage, Sunny holding on like he'd never held on in his life. Then, like the other plane before it, it tipped forward, ploughing the nose – with its already broken propeller – into the field.

Earth churned up everywhere.

Sheep bleated.

Mimi and Ace gasped.

Then, to their amazement, the whole plane flipped over on to its back, the tail end wedging itself in the "Y" of a tree.

What seemed so strange was how s-l-o-w-l-y it happened. The movement was almost like a graceful somersault...

...leaving Alphonso Tubb and Sunny hanging upside-down from their cockpits.

"Woweeeeeeeeeeeeeeeeeeeeeeeh!" cried Dr Tubb, face breaking into a grin. "Are you all right, Sunny?"

Sunny didn't reply. He laughed. It wasn't exactly a happy laugh, but they'd made it safely to the ground.

Without waiting for any orders, instructions or even words of encouragement, Fingers strode purposefully up to the plane and, with extraordinary gentleness, wrapped his trunk around upside-down Sunny.

Sunny gave another laugh. A happy one this time. "Fingers, am I glad to see you!" he said, unclipping his seatbelt. Now freed, the elephant carefully turned him the right way up and placed his feet on the ground. Sunny stumbled, but was still held in Fingers' trunk so managed to steady himself. "Thanks," he said.

A look passed between the elephant and boy. One of love and understanding. Fingers unwound his trunk and turned his attention to Alphonso Tubb, who'd wisely stayed put. If, say, Tubb had simply managed to unclip his seatbelt – which was easier said than done with his whole body weight straining on it anyway – he would've fallen to the ground head first and possibly broken his neck. As it was, he was more than happy for the elephant to turn him carefully upright and sit him on the grass.

"Thank you," said Dr Tubb, now that he was the right way up and back on good old solid ground. He had, of course, recognised Mimi and Ace the instant he'd laid eyes on them. They were busy with Sunny, who was trying to reassure them that he was OK.

"I'm fine now that I've got my feet back on

the ground," he said.

"What were you doing in the plane?" asked Dr Tubb.

"Hiding," said Sunny.

Dr Tubb was about to ask who from, when WingCo Fish strode over to greet them.

"Jeepers!" said Fish. "That was some landing." He looked at Tubb's wrecked plane. "For both of us."

"I was a bit worried when the wheels came off!" Mimi confessed. She pointed to the tree that had ripped them from the plane. They were still hanging from the branches. Everyone stared.

Just then, Jenny Prendergast came into view.

From the road she'd seen the plane containing her beloved Alphonso Tubb disappear behind the line of the hedge, and had instructed Norris to stop the van so that she could clamber over a gate and run across the sheep-filled field.

Kicking off her high-heeled shoes to speed herself up, she ran barefoot across the grass towards the plane. She let out a squeal of horror when she saw that it was upside down, swiftly followed by a squeal of delight when she saw her beloved Tubby was standing on his own two feet talking to a man and a group of children ... by an elephant.

"Tubby! My Tubby!" she shouted.

Now the others arrived from across the field. The "others" being people from the country fair who'd seen the plane going down and were coming to help. Or gawp.

Lady "La-La" Bigg had managed to commandeer a tractor, which was exactly the same red as the wing commander's plane, and was at the front of the crowd, driving it through the gap in the hedge created by Fingers, with Poppet the pig up in the cab at her side. Mrs Lunge's dog, Squat, was sitting on the roof.

"Is anyone hurt?" shouted her ladyship, bringing the tractor to a halt.

The pig jumped down from the tractor and excitedly trotted towards Fingers. I'd say *bounded* towards Fingers, but Poppet's plump body didn't really allow for much in the way of bounding.

Everyone crowded round the two men and the boy (with the funny ears, sticky-up hair and blue dress), who were quick to assure everyone that there were no bones broken. Then Jenny Prendergast finally reached Alphonso Tubb and the two threw their arms around each other.

"You're alive!" wailed Jenny.

"Very much so!" said the doctor. He pulled

back a little and looked her directly in the eyes. "Well?"

"Well what, Tubby dearest?" asked Jenny, stepping back.

"Well, what's your answer?" asked Alphonso Tubb. "Will you make me the happiest man alive? Will you marry me?"

Jenny did a little skip in the air, clapping her hands together. "Oh, yes, dearest Tubby! A thousand times, yes!"

They kissed. The crowd cheered.

There…

…was

…a

…howl.

"A A A A A A A A A A A A A A A OOOOOOOOOOOOOOO!"

It was the kind of howl you'd expect to be coming from a wolf with very bad toothache or its tail stuck in a lift door.

"AAAAAAAAAAAAAAAA
OOOOOOOOOOOOOOO!"

The crowd fell silent. Everyone looked in the direction of the noise. There stood Norris. Now *he* fell silent.

"OOO—"

He bowed his head.

Jenny skipped over to him and squeezed his hand. "Best of friends?" she asked.

Norris Bootle looked deep into her eyes. For a while, he didn't say anything. Finally he nodded. "Best of friends, old girl," he said, and gave her a best-of-friends kind of hug. Then Norris walked across the grass and shook Dr Tubb by the hand. "Congratulations," he said. "You're a very lucky man."

"Very lucky," agreed the doctor, and gave Jenny a more-than-just-best-of-friends kiss.

Just about everyone cheered again, no one louder than Sunny. You feel a certain bond with a man who safely lands an out-of-control plane you've accidentally ended up in, take my word for it. He couldn't wait to tell Mr and Mrs Grunt what had happened. But where were they? They weren't among the crowd. They were nowhere to be seen.

Chapter Ten

Melon Time !

To say that Mr Grunt was lucky might be a bit of an exaggeration because a lucky man wouldn't get chased by bees and end up tripping over a rope and setting off a load of fireworks including the prototype OOMPH 5, which in turn brought down a plane.

So no, Mr Grunt wasn't lucky in that sense, but he *was* lucky in the sense that he didn't end up getting stung by all the bees, however many there were. (He hadn't had a chance to guess the number, remember?)

After he'd tripped over and all the rockets had gone off, lit by Mr Lippy's flaming juggling club, the sudden flashes and loud noises had made the insects think twice about bugging the strange man with the great big plaster on his nose.

Instead, they suddenly veered away, in one great big living cloud, and decided to visit the tea tent instead, swarming in through the

open doorway and landing on a fine selection of cakes and pastries. The only person in there was soon *out* of there, screaming as he ran, but still managing to cling on to his Bakewell slice. (He was a cake-lover who wasn't about to surrender that in a hurry.)

Mr Grunt took this as an opportunity to escape, not least because an extraordinarily large and angry man wearing a T-shirt bearing the words PATTERSON'S PYROTECHNICS was lumbering towards him like a daddy bear, furious with someone for snatching away his baby bear's honey sandwich without asking.

Mr Grunt had no idea that "pyrotechnics"  meant the art of making and setting off fireworks, but he could tell when someone much bigger than him wasn't pleased to see him ... so he hauled himself up and started running again.

When he reached the caravan in the car park, he was surprised to see that Fingers had gone. He was also relieved to find that there was no sign of Mrs Grunt and Ma Lunge, so he decided to take the opportunity to have a quick nap.

First, he popped Clip and Clop back in their special trailer. They'd enjoyed their fill of flowers and were ready for a nap too. He was very fond of those old donkeys and chatted to them and patted them as he got them aboard.

He was just making his way up the stairs to bed when Ma Lunge appeared in the doorway of the caravan.

"Bother," he grunted.

"There you are," sighed Mrs Lunge, plonking her huge handbag down on the top step beside her. "I suppose it was you who shot down that plane?"

"What are you talking about?" he said. He turned his back on Mrs Lunge and went to climb the remaining stairs. "I've been busy with bees."

"You, as busy as a bee? I don't believe a word of it," said the tiny woman. "You're one of nature's layabouts."

Mr Grunt stopped on the stairs a second time, turned back around and glared down at her. "I didn't say that I was as busy *as* a bee, I said that I was busy *with* bees. I was being chased by them."

"And why would bees want to chase you, of all people?" asked Mrs Lunge. "You hardly look like a pretty flower!"

"More like a dustbin," said Mrs Grunt, who was now climbing up the caravan steps and joining in the conversation from the doorway.

"Tree surgeon!" snapped Mr Grunt.

"Trowel!" shouted Mrs Grunt.

"Pig iron!"

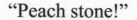

"Peach stone!"

"Bat's wing!"

"Fridge magnet!"

"Fridge magnet?" Mr Grunt smiled. He was glad she was back. "What have you two been doing?" he asked. "You've been gone a long time."

"I was trying to make sure that Ma beat Edna Tuppenny in the Preserves, Jams and Jellies Competition," said Mrs Grunt, "by sabotaging Edna's efforts."

"And I was also trying to make sure that I won the Preserves, Jams and Jellies Competition," said Mrs Lunge.

"And?" said Mr Grunt.

"And what?" asked Mrs Grunt and her mother.

"And what went wrong?"

"Who says anything went wrong?" said Mrs

Grunt indignantly.

"Well, it did, didn't it?" asked Mr Grunt.

"Yes," said Mrs Grunt.

"I've been disqualified," sighed Mrs Lunge.

"For life," her daughter added.

"HA!" said Mr Grunt, then laughed so much that he fell down the stairs.

While Mr Grunt lay on the sofa, Mrs Grunt held a soothing half-a-melon to the bump on her husband's head, and told him about being caught red-handed putting a dead fly in

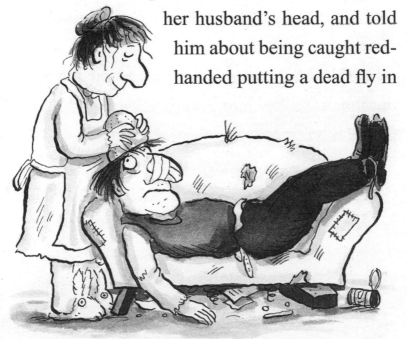

one of Edna Tuppenny's jars, and about her ma emerging, moments later, from beneath the table.

"You're useless, you are!" Mr Grunt laughed.

Ma Lunge sighed. "It's not my day. The drought... The disqualification... *And* I lost my purse."

"If you need money, you just ask me," said Mr Grunt. "I'll give you money. We're family."

He dug his hand in his pocket and pulled out the purse, holding it up in the air from his position lying on the sofa.

Mrs Grunt's mum was surprised for three reasons:

1. She was surprised by Mr Grunt's sudden and unexpected generosity. Usually, getting him to give her money was like trying to talk a brick wall into taking off its trousers. And brick walls don't even wear trousers.*
(*Which is the point.)
2. She was surprised by this talk of her being "family". Mr Grunt rarely wanted anything to do with her.
3. She was surprised to discover that it was her *own* purse.

"So you're the one who stole it," sighed Mrs Lunge. "I might have known."

"Who says I didn't just find it?" he demanded.

"Well, *did* you just find Ma's purse?" demanded Mrs Grunt.

"Yes."

"Where?"

"In her handbag."

"Good work, mister!" grinned Mrs Grunt.

"Thank you, wife!" said Mr Grunt.

"I want a cup of tea *now*!" said Ma Lunge. She stuffed her purse back in her handbag, and shut the clasp with a loud "CLICK!"

The Grunts heard the others returning to the country fair across the fields before they saw them. It's hard to be quiet with a tractor, an excited squealing pig, an equally-excited Lady "La-La" Bigg, a trumpeting elephant, a yappy dog, some children (one of whom had escaped an almost plane-crash) and an accompanying crowd of stallholders and visitors, all jabbering away, discussing what they saw and heard and what might have happened as well as what actually *did*.

Dr Tubb and Jenny Prendergast were sitting on top of Fingers. He, the returning hero. She, the newly engaged fiancée. WingCo Fish was squeezed into the tractor cab with her ladyship.

A dejected Norris Bootle, meanwhile, was driving his van back down the lane alone. He knew that once the initial relief of finding her beloved Tubby was unharmed had worn off, and she'd got used to the idea of actually being engaged to the doctor, she could concentrate on being VERY annoyed with him for all the trouble he'd caused.

"What a racket!" said Mrs Grunt. She'd had enough of holding the half-a-melon to Mr Grunt's head. She opened the top of the caravan's stable door and chucked it out into the car park.

The half-a-melon narrowly missed a man holding a book of raffle tickets but did manage to hit a very large man in the chest. He was wearing a T-shirt bearing the words PATTERSON'S PYROTECHNICS.

The letters were now splattered with old melon and pips.

The man didn't seem very happy about it. He looked down, brushed the front of his T-shirt with his huge, hairy hand – his fingers the size of sausages – licked the melon juice from it and GLARED.

With the beekeeper on one side of him and a policeman on the other, he lumbered towards the Grunts' caravan like an angry daddy bear furious with someone for setting off his baby bear's fireworks without asking...

Mrs Grunt suspected that she was imagining it, but she was pretty sure she'd just seen steam coming out of his ears.

"Mister?" she shouted, slamming the top of the stable door behind her and pulling across the large bolt. "We've got company!"

Chapter Eleven
Six is a Crowd

When the policeman came up the caravan steps and banged on the door, Mrs Grunt's first instinct was for them all to hide. "We can pretend not to be here!" she shouted.

"Didn't you say you just hit one of them with half a melon?" snorted Mr Grunt.

"Yes—"

"And they must have seen you slam the door."

"Yes, but—"

"But what?" demanded Mr Grunt.

"But… Buttery biscuit base!" said Mrs Grunt with a very impressive snort. She lifted the seat of the sofa to see if she could hide herself inside, but it was already crammed full of stuff. "HUMPH!" she muttered.

Mr Grunt's first instinct wasn't to hide but to escape through a window. The one he knew that he could easily fit through was the window in the bedroom – because he regularly fell out of it – but, in his haste to escape, he tried squeezing through the downstairs one at the side.

He got stuck.

The policeman meanwhile was knocking very

loudly on the door. He started off by saying, "Open the door, please!"

This was soon followed by, "I know you're in there!"

Then – by the time the knocking had turned to banging the door with the side of his fist – he was shouting, "Open up in the name of the Law!" He was saying "Law!" with a capital "L," which meant that there must be no more messing about.

By the time Ma Lunge finally slid back the bolt and opened the door, Mrs Grunt had just managed to free Mr Grunt and pull him back into the room by his belt. His belt – made from two old belts sewn together – had broken in the process. Mrs Grunt was left holding the pieces, while Mr Grunt was left holding his trousers up.

He found himself not only face to face

with an officer of the law but also two of his accusers: the beekeeper and the man from Patterson's Pyrotechnics. In fact, it was getting rather crowded. The pyrotechnics man was SO large that he not only had to duck his head but bend sideways too, one shoulder lower than the other, to be able to stand up in the caravan. Under other circumstances Mr and Mrs Grunt would probably have laughed and pointed. On this occasion they didn't.

One reason for this might have been that Mrs Grunt had, meanwhile, got down on her hands and knees and was pretending to be a table (and tables don't laugh). She'd even managed to rest Chocolate Biscuit, her cat-shaped doorstop, on top of her, to look like a table ornament.

"Are you all right, madam?" asked the policeman with a puzzled frown.

"PERFECTLY!" said Mrs Grunt, struggling to her feet. Chocolate Biscuit fell off and landed on Mr Grunt's toe.

"OUCH!" he bellowed, grabbing his foot. This meant his letting go of his waistband so – beltless – his trousers fell round his ankles. "What are you playing at, wife?" he demanded, pulling his trousers up and tucking them into the top of his pants to try to keep them from falling down again.

"I was simply inspecting a stain on the carpet," she said, pointing at nothing.

"Good," said the policeman, for something to say. "Now, I need to ask you both a series of questions but before we go any further I'm going to ask this gentleman –" he nodded at the giant in the T-shirt, "– to formally identify you."

"I don't need anyone to formally identify

me. I know very well who I am," said Mr Grunt. It was true. He didn't even need a mirror.

"He's idiot-chops," said Mrs Grunt helpfully. "That's who *he* is."

"Lip-balm!"

"Monkey nut!"

"Child lock!"

"Water-cooler!"

The policeman put up his hand for silence. "Please!" he said.

"I'm Mr Grunt," said Mr Grunt.

"I need Mr Smith—"

Mr Grunt's eyes narrowed as he looked up at the Patterson's Pyrotechnics man. "No one's really called Smith!" he said.

"Well, I am," said Mr Smith.

"Then who's Patterson?" demanded Mrs Grunt, who'd picked up Chocolate Biscuit and now had him tucked under her arm. "Did you steal that T-shirt, you ... you ... T-shirt thief!" She gave a triumphant grunt.

"Mr Patterson is my boss," said Mr Smith. His voice was deep.

"Before we go any further," said the policeman, a little louder this time, "I need Mr Smith here to formally identify you as the man who set off the fireworks."

"Yes, that's him," said Mr Smith.

"By 'him' you mean Mr Grunt?" asked the policeman. He was writing things down in his notebook.

"Yes," said Mr Smith.

"Of course he means him," said Mrs Grunt. "I don't see any other Misters in here except you, mister." She prodded the policeman. One should never prod a policeman or a policewoman. They don't like being prodded.

"I'm simply following Official Procedure, madam," he said, making a don't-even-THINK-of-prodding-me-again face. "It's the way that things have to be done to stand up in a court of law."

"What if you want to sit down in a court of law?" demanded Mr Grunt. "HA! Answer me that."

The policeman chose to ignore Mr Grunt or at least try to, though it wasn't as easy as it sounds. "Madam," he said to the beekeeper. "Can you confirm that Mr Grunt is the man who stole your bees?"

"What if you want to lie down in a court of law?" demanded Mrs Grunt this time. "What if you want to float by on a lilo in a court of law? Or you just want to swing by and say 'Hi!'?" She made a sound like the victory cry of the bull ape (better known as the cry Tarzan makes when he swings through the jungle on those vines of his).

The policeman repeated the question. "Was this man, calling himself Mr Grunt, the man who stole your bees?"

"He tried to, yes," said the beekeeper.

"Thank you," said the policeman, scribbling further notes in his little black notebook. "Then I must ask you to leave so that I can now conduct an—"

"Orchestra?" suggested Mrs Grunt.

"A thorough search?" suggested Mr Grunt.

"An ostrich?" suggested Mrs Grunt.

Mr Grunt spluttered. "Don't be ridiculous, wife. He can't conduct an ostrich."

"Can."

"Can't."

"Can."

"Can't."

"Can if it's an ostrich *in the orchestra*," said Mrs Grunt, looking VERY pleased with herself indeed.

Mr Grunt gave Mrs Grunt a loving hug. "That's my girl!" he beamed.

Mr Smith ducked back through the doorway and out of the caravan, closely followed by the beekeeper.

"Can we sit down?" the policeman asked Mr Grunt. "I have a great many questions."

"If you must," Mr Grunt grunted. "What was it you were going to conduct?"

"An interview," said the policeman. "Hence the questions."

Over the next hour, Mr Grunt was accused of having done many things that day from "endangering aircraft" to "actual bodily harm to a public convenience".

One of the few things Mr Grunt *wasn't* charged with was stealing Mr Lippy's juggling torch. The clown didn't want to press charges.

The man with the raffle tickets *had* wanted Mr Grunt to be charged for parking in a NO PARKING area and for letting his "mules" – he didn't know a pair of donkeys when he saw one – eat a display of prize-winning flowers, but the police didn't seem interested.

There was also the matter of *Mrs* Grunt having tampered with Edna Tuppenny's jars in the Preserves, Jams and Jellies Competition. She might very well have been poisoning them. And, not only that, if Mrs Grunt's mother, Mrs Lunge, had won the contest, and there was a cash prize as well as a certificate and cup, then wouldn't that be classed as *obtaining money by deception*?

The policeman might well have decided not to pursue the matter of the Preserves, Jams and Jellies Competition if Mrs Grunt hadn't suddenly decided it was a good idea to bite his ankle.

He yelped.

"That'll teach you!" she cackled.

The policeman turned to a fresh page in his notebook, wrote down her name and started to write. The first line was, "intent to poison".

Chapter Twelve

In a Jam

The Grunts were in a jam, or, to be more accurate, they were in a holding cell underneath a courtroom. It looked rather like those jails you see in Westerns: like a cage of metal bars where only the outer wall is made of stone.

Sunny was in the cell with Mr and Mrs Grunt rather like in the picture on the cover of this book except, of course, Mr Grunt had his nose in a bandage.*

[*EDITOR'S NOTE: A picture on the cover

showing Mr Grunt with a nose bandage would be enough to put most readers off, which is why there isn't a nose-bandage in sight.]

The policeman in charge of the cells hadn't wanted to let Sunny in until Mr Grunt had explained that he was their lawyer.

"And you have to let our lawyer in."

"He's your lawyer? He looks very young to be a lawyer," said the policeman with a frown. He was wondering who in their right mind would hire such a young lawyer with such wonky ears, such sticky-up hair and wearing such an odd blue dress. Then he looked at Mr and Mrs Grunt.

Yup. That made sense.

"OK then," said the policeman, letting Sunny into the holding cell. "Name?"

"Sorry?" asked Sunny.

"I need your name for the ledger, sir." He pointed at an official-looking book on his desk in the corridor that the cell doors opened out on to. "So the court knows who'll be representing them at the hearing."

"Ah," said Sunny. They hadn't thought this through. There was no way he could actually act as a lawyer in any court case!

"Sunny," said Mrs Grunt. "He's called Sunny."

"Sunny," said the policeman. He began writing in the ledger.

"With a 'u'," said Sunny, because he knew some people spelled Sunny as "Sonny" with an "o".

"Sunny Withayew," said the policeman as he wrote, thinking the last part was Sunny's surname, not a spelling instruction. He put down his pen and selected a key from the chain hanging from his belt, and unlocked the cell door. "OK, Mr Withayew, in you go."

"So what happens now?" asked Sunny as the door was locked behind him.

"We'll tell the judge to let us go," said Mr Grunt. He was busy tucking his shirt into the top of his trousers. (He'd fixed the belt with an old office stapler he'd managed to "borrow" off a policeman's desk as they were being bundled into the cells.)

"Dad," said Sunny, then lowered his voice in case the policeman heard. (Lawyers probably didn't generally call their clients "Dad".) "If you're going up in front of the judge tomorrow, do you have any idea what you're going to say?"

"All we have to do is tell the truth, the whole truth and nothing but—"

"A tin of coconut milk?" suggested Mrs Grunt.

Mr Grunt grunted. "I'll tell 'em I was having a fun day out and might have bumped into a few people and a few things. That's all."

"Shouldn't you have a *real* lawyer, Dad?" said Sunny.

"Lawyers are expensive!" said Mr Grunt.

"And noisy," added Mrs Grunt.

"You're thinking of lawnmowers," said Mr Grunt.

"Am not."

"Are."

"Not."

"Are."

"I was thinking of volcanoes. They're noisy," said Mrs Grunt.

"Not always," said Mr Grunt. "Not the quiet ones. HA!"

"But Lady Bigg told me that if you can't afford your own lawyer, the court will provide one for you."

"What does that mean?" demanded Mrs Grunt.

"It means that they pay for your lawyer. You don't have to," Sunny explained. "The only catch is, you get who you're given…"

"Which is me!" said a man, striding down the corridor into view.

"Who are you?" asked the puzzled policeman.

The man looked familiar to Sunny but at the same time *un*familiar. It was Sack, the ex-gardener from Bigg Manor! But Sack unlike they'd ever seen him before. He was dressed in a shiny blue suit and tie and was carrying a brand-new briefcase.

When Sunny and the Grunts first went to Bigg Manor, Mimi was still the boot boy and Sack was still the gardener. But with Lord Bigg in jail, Lady Bigg had freed the servants of all their duties and Sack was thrilled, delighted and over the moon that he never had to plant another bulb, prune another rose, trim another bush or grow another seedling. He hated gardening. What he yearned to be was an inventor.

And Sack had invented some amazing things. He invented the bath plug and the necktie. The front-door bell and the bicycle. He invented inflatable dolphins and egg cups.

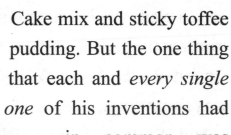

Cake mix and sticky toffee pudding. But the one thing that each and *every single one* of his inventions had in common was that someone had invented it before him. So he gave up on the dream of being a professional inventor, left Bigg Manor (where all the ex-servants, except Peach the former butler, still chose to live) and went to night school TO BECOME A LAWYER.

215

He loved it. He learned to be a lawyer at night and did lots of lawyering homework during the day. And he found that he was really rather good at it. He ended up doing something called the A.L.P. which stands for the Accelerated Law Programme. It meant that he became a lawyer *very quickly indeed*. And he was about to find out just how good he really was or wasn't, because Mr and Mrs Grunt were to be his first clients in his first ever court hearing!

"Who am I?" Sack asked the puzzled policeman. "I'm Sack the court-appointed lawyer."

"Then who's *he*?" demanded the policeman.

"He's our lawyer too," said Mr Grunt, with a grunt. "Two of us. Two lawyers. What's the problem?"

"Precisely," said Sack, who had no idea

what was going on but was having the time of his life. "So if you'd be kind enough to leave us alone with our clients…"

"Just as soon as I have your name in my ledger, sir," said the policeman. He wrote it down, then, as good as his word, he left the corridor, closing the door behind him.

"Right!" said Sack. "Let's get down to business!"

Sunny had never seen Sack look so happy.

"Don't waste your time with all that," said Mr Grunt. "Whatever it is that they say I've done, I'm innocent. I took Mrs Grunt's mother to the country fair, that's all. The rest is—"

"Porridge!" said Mrs Grunt.

"The rest is not porridge, you dust ball!"

"Harpoon!"

"Cashback!"

"Sandpit!"

"The rest is hogwash. I didn't do a single thing they say I did."

"And it'll be my job to make sure you don't rot in jail!" said Sack, pulling up a stool and sitting himself in front of the bars of the cell.

"Don't you need time to prepare for the trial?" asked Sunny.

"Tomorrow isn't a trial," said Sack, pulling a buff-coloured file stuffed with papers out of his case. "Tomorrow's a hearing. It's to decide if either or both of you have a case to answer." He shut the briefcase, resting it on his lap like a tray and placing the fat file on top of it. "In other words, all the charges may get thrown out tomorrow and you won't even have to go to trial."

"Or?" asked Sunny.

"Or they may decide that there *will* be a trial. In which case, we'll agree a date and then they'll set you free as long as you turn up on the day." Sack suddenly looked a little hesitant.

"Or?" asked Sunny. Again.

"Or they may decide that there'll be a trial and that one or both of you will need to stay in jail until – er – then," said Sack. "It all depends how it goes upstairs tomorrow." He pointed up at the ceiling of the holding cells, above which was the floor of the courtroom.

"How do you think it'll go?" asked Sunny through the bars.

"Have no fear," said Sack. "I'm on the case!"

Sunny might have felt more confident if he hadn't already noticed what was written on the pages in Sack's impressively fat buff-coloured folder, sitting on the briefcase on his knee.

Nothing.

The pages were totally blank.

Chapter Thirteen

Silence in Court!

It was the morning of Mr and Mrs Grunt's hearing and the courtroom was packed. Lady "La-La" Bigg had managed to squeeze all those she needed to into her rusty old car: Peach, the former butler who now ran her pub, The Happy Pig, Agnes the former cook and maid, Agnes' husband Jack, the former handyman (also known as Former Handyman Jack,) and Poppet the pig.

The car was tiny. Peach sat in the front next to Lady Bigg, sitting as upright and as

dignified as possible, but with his knees up
to his chin. This was because he'd moved his
seat as far forward as it would go to make
room behind. Agnes and Jack sat in the back,
Poppet the pig between them. Because of the
way the car roof sloped, Jack could only fit in
the car if he had his head and one elbow out
of the window. Agnes had folded herself up
as much as possible, like a piece of human

origami. Poppet had the most room and seemed as happy as a pig in a car with four people.

Lady Bigg pulled the tiny car to a halt in one of the few remaining spaces in the courtroom car park and everyone spilled out, stretching their legs, rolling their heads, bending and stretching and generally trying to get some feeling back into their limbs.

Jack the former handyman's neck made a terrible "CLICK" and got stuck sideways, so he walked towards the courthouse as though he were still sticking his head out of a car window, but an imaginary one this time. Peach pushed Poppet the pig in a pushchair.

Once inside, Lady Bigg's group made their way to the public gallery, the place where members of the public could sit upstairs in rows and look down on proceedings below (a

bit like at a theatre). There was a sign at the
entrance to the gallery that clearly stated:

NO PIGS

This was why Lady "La-La" Bigg had given
Poppet rouged cheeks, red lipstick, a rather
ill-fitting floral dress, and a sunhat. This was
why Peach was pushing her along in the large,
old-fashioned pushchair.

"Mornin', your ladyship," said Mr Harper, the courthouse security guard, touching the peak of his cap in respect. Lady Bigg was a well-known figure in the neighbourhood, not least because she was the lady of the manor – though she actually lived in a pigsty – and because she was a little – er – eccentric.

"Good morning, Harper!" said Lady "La-La" Bigg. She and her ex-servants formed a sort of human shield between him and the pig as they walked merrily on.

Six seats in the front row of the public gallery had been reserved for "Lady Bigg's party" (the five in the car and one for Mimi). The humans occupied four of them, but two remained empty: one for Mimi when she came up to the gallery, and Poppet's because she remained in the pushchair at the end of the row. Lady Bigg sat next to her, rubbing the pig's tummy to keep her contented. On the other side of the aisle sat Lara Farp, Ace, Dr Alphonso Tubb and Jenny Prendergast. Most of them were leaning over the edge of the gallery to look at the courtroom below.

Two rows behind Lady Biggs sat a very petite woman with golden hair who, you may not be surprised to learn, had won the southern heat of the Miss Dainty Lady Shopkeeper Contest on a number of occasions. She was holding a broom handle on to which she'd nailed a handwritten placard bearing the words:

THROW THEM BOTH IN PRISON, THEN THROW AWAY THE KEY.

It was none other than Mrs Winterbottom of Hall's Groceries.

Down in the holding cells, Sack (their court-appointed lawyer) and Sunny Withayew (the Grunt-appointed pretend-lawyer) were having some last-minute discussions with their clients.

"So we're all agreed then," said Sack, snapping his briefcase shut.

"On what?" asked Mrs Grunt.

"That, to get the judge to free you, you need to make a good impression," Sack reminded them.

Mrs Grunt started hissing. "Hsssssssssssssss. That's my impression of a punctured beach ball!" she cackled.

"Behave!" grunted Mr Grunt.

"Beehive!" said Mrs Grunt, then realising how clever she'd been – what with bees having played a major part in how they'd ended up here – she started to buzz.

A door opened at the end of the corridor, and there was Mimi. She came hurrying in, Frizzle and Twist flitting around her head.

"I just want to wish you good luck, Mr and Mrs Grunt," she said. She gave Sunny a hug. "Lady Bigg and the others are up in the public gallery. Just about everyone from the manor's here, as well as Lara Farp and Ace."

"That's excellent!" said Sack, rubbing his hands. "Moral support!"

"I'd better get up there," said Mimi. She turned to Sack. "All set?"

"All set, Mimi," nodded Sack. He patted his briefcase.

Both Mimi and Sunny had serious doubts.

By the time Mr and Mrs Grunt were brought

up from the holding cells, the courtroom was packed. Not only was the public gallery full, but the various court officials were in place: the clerk of the court, the court recorder (who'd write everything down), the defence "lawyers", Sack and Sunny, and the prosecution lawyer, Mr Benderby. And then there was the judge, Judge Humperdink.

More than anything, Judge Humperdink's head looked like a balloon. It was smooth and hairless and even shaped like one. His ears were tiny, and his small eyes, small nose and small  mouth were all neatly clustered together as though someone had drawn all his features in the middle of a balloon rather than using up the available space.

His voice was high-pitched, like someone who'd swallowed helium.

If Sack had been an experienced lawyer, he'd have known about Judge Humperdink and would have warned the Grunts that, though he looked funny and sounded even funnier, they mustn't laugh and point and make rude jokes about him *because judges don't like that kind of thing*. (It's possibly even WORSE than prodding a police officer.)

So the first thing Mr and Mrs Grunt did when they were led up into the dock – a bit like a waist-high wooden box with walls on three sides and steps at the back – was to look at Judge Humperdink directly opposite them, then look at each other and burst out laughing.

"Oi, balloon face..." said Mr Grunt.

I wish I could say that Judge Humperdink banged his gavel, one of those little hammers you often see judges hitting their desks with in films and cartoons, but he didn't have one.

"Silence in court!" said the clerk of the court, who was standing next to the judge's podium, a raised area where the judge could sit and look down on the accused (in this case the Grunts).

Now the judge spoke. "First and foremost, I'd like to remind everyone that this is not a trial. It is a hearing to decide whether there are cases to be answered and if there is a *need* for a trial." He looked directly at Mr Grunt. "Is that clear, Mr Grunt?"

"As jelly," nodded Mr Grunt.

"Is that clear, Mrs Grunt?" Humperdink squeaked.

"As what he said," said Mrs Grunt.

Judge Humperdink frowned.

"My clients understand, your honour," said Sack grandly.

So the hearing began. The first charge Mr Grunt had to answer was *vandalism: deliberately sitting on a guess-the-weight cake.*

"I remember it was squishy," said Mr Grunt.

"Because you squashed it," said Mr Benderby for the prosecution.

"It looked badly made and flat," said Mr Grunt.

"Because you squashed it," said Mr

Benderby for the prosecution.

"Why are you picking on me, big ears?" asked Mr Grunt.

Judge Humperdink glared at Mr Grunt and would, I AM SURE, have banged his gavel if he'd had one. "It's his job, Mr Grunt!" he squeaked.

Sack got up and stared at a blank piece of paper in his hand. "Do you deny sitting on the cake, Mr Grunt?"

"Of course not," said Mr Grunt indignantly. "I did sit on it."

"Big bum," said Mrs Grunt.

"Bedpan!" said Mr Grunt.

"Your honour, the reason why my client sat on the cake was because the cake was placed at the height of a seat," said Sack, hurriedly interrupting the Grunts before they had a full-on slanging match. "The guess-the-weight cake was placed on a table below regulation height, putting it at seating level and, therefore, officially making it a seat, according to…"

He paused, looked down and pointed to a blank piece of paper on the desk in front of Sunny, who was sitting to his right. Sunny passed him the blank piece of paper, which Sack then looked at as though referring to important notes.

"…according to the Public Crouching, Lounging and Seating Act of 1892. So I would submit that there is no case to answer!"

Judge Humperdink was clearly impressed by the lawyer's deep knowledge of the law.

If truth be told, Humperdink had rather given up on keeping up with the law in recent years. When he was a younger judge he'd loved reading big, fat, juicy leather-bound law books. Nowadays he much preferred to hum and look out of the window, or imagine that the gravy stains on his ties were islands. He'd give these islands names and then think about who might live on them, or where they'd set up the fish market. Humperdink thought it was very useful that this bright new lawyer from the Accelerated Law Programme was up to date with all this stuff – and clearly remembered all the older laws too – so that he didn't have to be.

"No case to answer?" Judge Humperdink asked Sack.

"That is my belief, your honour," said Sack.

"Agreed," said the judge.

There was a cheer from someone. Mr Grunt
hugged Mrs Grunt. Mrs Grunt hugged Mr
Grunt.

"Right then, we'll be off," said Mr Grunt,
turning to leave.

"Silence in court!" shouted the clerk of the

court, because that was pretty much all he ever got to say and he *liked* saying it.

"Control your clients, Mr Sack and Mr Withayew!" said the judge. He didn't only need knowledgeable lawyers to make his life easier. He needed ones who could make their clients behave. "Mr and Mrs Grunt, this is just the *first* of the charges put to you. There are many more still to answer." Humperdink hoped this wouldn't take too long. He was planning to have soup for lunch – that was bound to mean more stains on his tie, more imaginary islands to visit and more fish markets to position.

Then came the next charge. *Criminal damage: smashing a quantity of locally-made-lovingly-made-home-made pottery.*

"Yup, that was me," said Mr Grunt. "Tripped and smashed the lot of it. Ugly stuff."

"It is irrelevant whether or not the pottery was ugly," said Mr Benderby for the prosecution.

"Not if you had it on your sideboard," said Mrs Grunt. "Someone might come in and say, 'What hideous pottery!'"

"Ugly!"

"Disgusting!"

"Sickening!"

"Downright horrible!"

"This is irrelevant!" repeated Mr Benderby.

"He's picking on my husband again, Your Judgementship!" said Mrs Grunt.

"IT'S HIS JOB, MRS GRUNT," said Judge Humperdink, raising his voice a little more than was truly necessary.

Sack cleared his throat. "Your honour, it was in fact the pottery that was at fault, not my client. It was a potential danger to the public with its jagged edges, should it break. It was a dangerous accident *waiting to happen.* It should have been stored in such a way to prevent it being a potential hazard to country-fair-goers..." He paused.

Sunny, warming to his role, shuffled around a few more sheets of blank paper on the table in front of him before picking up one and passing it to Sack, who pretended to read from it.

"... as laid out in the Safe Display of Items Which Can Get Pointy Or Sharp If Broken Act of 1922. Once again, I beg to suggest that there is no case to answer!"

"Agreed!" said Judge Humperdink, though he looked far from pleased about it and glared at Mr Benderby of the prosecution.

A much happier look passed between Sunny from the bench where he was seated and Mimi up in the gallery. Ace, meanwhile, let out a little cheer.

"Silence in court!" shouted the clerk of the court, delighted to have an opportunity to say it again. (If truth be told, he was secretly hoping for even *more* cheering.)

Mrs Winterbottom looked glum and shook her placard in polite silence.

THROW THEM BOTH IN PRISON, THEN THROW AWAY THE KEY.

Judge Humperdink was getting more than a little fed up with these interruptions. The more interrupting, the longer he would have to wait for his soup. And the longer the judge would have to wait for his soup, the longer he would have to wait for fresh soup stains on his tie. Humperdink looked down at the next charge on the sheet: *sabotaging a knitting machine and wasting wool*. Now, surely THAT was something Mr Grunt couldn't deny or wriggle out of? And nobody liked a wool-waster!

"The knitting machine in question is of such a size and power that the National Union of Knitting requires that it be attended by one of their members at *all* times if used in a public area, including fair grounds or trade shows," said Sack patiently. "As everyone in this courtroom knows, with great knitting comes great responsibility—"

He was interrupted by a loud "Hear! Hear!" from an elderly gentleman in the public gallery, who was busy knitting a cosy for his son's bicycle.

His son was the clerk of the court, who now called out, "Silence in court, Dad!"

Such was the silence that followed, all that could be heard was the click-clack of

241

knitting needles.

"Please continue, Mr Sack," said Judge Humperdink.

"Thank you, your honour," said the ex-gardener. "It was because the knitting machine was illegally left unattended that my client, Mr Grunt, had the opportunity to express his artistic temperament by creating the very long scarf indeed—"

"No case to answer!" Sunny interrupted, excitement getting the better of him.

"I am inclined to agree," squeaked Humperdink, who was beginning to get rather annoyed with Mr Benderby and the prosecution for bringing the charges in the first place. He was hoping that the courthouse canteen would serve a thick brown soup today. Brown soup made the best tie stains.

He looked down at the charge sheet and

sighed. Oh dear! Now, here was a charge that Mr Grunt and his hotshot lawyer team would find almost impossible to wriggle out of: *blowing up a public toilet.*

"Do you admit to filling it with lighted fireworks, Mr Grunt?" demanded Mr Benderby.

"Well, I'd hardly used unlighted ones, now, would I?" said Mr Grunt. "Numbskull."

"Trout net!" added Mrs Grunt.

"Kiwi fruit!"

"Sausage skin!"

Although the insults were directed at the lawyer for the prosecution, Mrs Grunt was so used to throwing them at Mr Grunt that she kicked her husband for good measure.

"OUCH!" he yelled.

"Silence in court!" said the clerk of the court and Mrs Grunt at exactly the same time, her in a sing-song voice. That made him AND the judge very angry.

"Mr Sack! Mr Withayew!" said Judge Humperdink. "If you cannot control your clients I will hold them in contempt of court!" And, from the way that he said it, even Sunny could tell that "contempt of court" was *not* a good thing.

Sack gave Mr and Mrs Grunt a warning glare, which was a bit like glaring at a bag of rice for all the good it did.

"Your honour," said Sack. "The Provision of Public Conveniences Act, 1977, gives a visitor to an outdoor attraction the right of access to a free-flowing toilet with flushing facilities and the right to unblock said toilets should they become unusable, *by any means necessary*... So I would suggest that there is no case to answer!"

Whereas before, those in the front row of public gallery had been fearful for the Grunts' future, it was now beginning to look like they might even be backing a winning team.

"Go, Sack, go!" muttered Lady "La-La" Bigg.

"Oink!" went Poppet.

"You tell 'em, Sack!" said Mimi under her breath.

Next came the charge of *bee rustling* (like cattle rusting but stealing bees not cattle).

"The bees were after my client. He wasn't after the bees," said Sack, getting a bit theatrical.

"No case to answer!" shouted Mrs Grunt.

"No place like home!" shouted Mr Grunt.

"No place for gnomes!" shouted Mrs Grunt.

Judge Humperdink looked like his head might POP. "This is my final warning, Mr and Mrs Grunt –" he said. He then turned his attention to Sack. "As for the bee rustling, however, I agree, Mr Sack. No case to answer."

A few people actually started to clap in response to this one, but the clerk of the court gave them the benefit of his very serious clerk-of-the-court stare, which he'd been taught at Day One of Clerk of the Court School, and they fell silent.

Next came the *unlicensed setting-off of fireworks*.

"This was clearly an accident resulting from Mr Grunt being chased by bees and trying to fend them off with a smoking juggling club and, what's more, an accident made possible by the poor safety measures taken by Mr Smith of Patterson's Pyrotechnics," said Sack.

From his seated position to Sack's right, Sunny grabbed a piece of blank paper from the desk and thrust it into Sack's hand. The ex-gardener-cum-almost-lawyer obviously had no use for it so, after a split second, he blew his nose on it, crumpled it up and thrust it in a trouser pocket. "I say, no case to answer!" he said.

"Agreed," sighed Judge Humperdink.

The prosecution lawyer, Mr Benderby, really looked as if he might cry.

Next up was the charge of *destruction of the prototype of the OOMPH 5 firework rocket*.

"Being a prototype, this rocket should never have been part of any public display! It hadn't undergone all the official safety tests required for it to be launched outside test conditions, under the Fireworks and Loud Bangs Act, 1998," said Sack. "Mr Grunt can't be blamed for what was accidental damage to something that shouldn't have been there in the first place. I therefore suggest … no case to answer!"

Now even Mr and Mrs Grunt had fallen silent…

Sack felt amazing. This was the best day of

his life! This was even better than the day he'd quit gardening! And Sunny was caught up in the whole excitement too. He didn't feel like a real lawyer, of course, but he was beginning to feel like a real lawyer's assistant!

Endangering aircraft and birdlife?

"It was the illegal OOMPH 5 that hit that aeroplane, not Mr Grunt."

"NO CASE TO ANSWER!" shouted just about everyone in the public gallery as one. Then they stomped their feet, or jumped up and cheered. Everyone, that is, but Miss

Winterbottom, of course. She felt something battering her knee and looked down to see a mighty small woman with a mighty big handbag. She was hitting her with it.

It was Mrs Lunge.

Sunny had left his grandmother back in the caravan, but Mrs Lunge had had other ideas.

Mimi was grinning from ear to ear and gave Sunny and Sack a double-handed thumbs-up. It was all going better than they could ever have hoped for.

What could possibly go wrong?

Chapter Fourteen

It Ain't Over

And so it was that the amazing Sack, an ex-gardener who hated gardening, demolished each and every single one of Mr Benderby's charges against Mr Grunt.

When Judge Humperdink announced that Mr Grunt didn't have a single case to answer and was free to go, a huge cheer went up throughout the courthouse and a delighted clerk of the court got to shout, "Silence in court!" three times, each time more loudly than the last. Humperdink was delighted because, with all these charges so expertly dismissed, he'd probably be sitting in front of a bowl of soup far sooner than he'd imagined.

It was only when Mr Grunt turned and left the dock, and Mrs Grunt turned to follow her husband but found her way blocked by a policewoman, that all fell quiet.

"Not you, I'm afraid, Mrs Grunt," said Sack. "You're still facing your charges."

The court went suddenly silent. In all the excitement, even Sunny had forgotten that his mum had two charges to answer. The clerk of the court read them out: *attempted poisoning* and *attempting to obtain money by deception.*

A different kind of hush descended upon the public gallery. This was serious stuff. Far more serious than ripping a glass roof off a hive of bees, it seemed.

Even Judge Humperdink's mood changed.

The tiny features on his balloon-shaped head suddenly looked very grave indeed.

Sack would really have to do something pretty magical to save Mrs Grunt from jail. He cleared his throat and straightened his tie.

"Your honour," said Mr Benderby for the prosecution. "We now come to the most serious charges of the day, that Mrs Grunt not only placed foreign objects in jellies, jams and preserves belonging to one Edna Tuppenny—"

"Edna the witch!" cried a voice from the gallery. No prizes for guessing which handbag-clutching, orange-toenailed onlooker shouted *that*.

Mr Benderby chose to ignore the interruption. "– but, as she believed that by doing such a thing she increased the chances of her mother winning the competition and the prize money, then the charge of attempting to obtain money by deception also stands."

"That's theft, that is!" shouted Edna Tuppenny in her lizard voice.

"Your honour—" began Sack, but Judge Humperdink put up his hand for silence. He was being handed a folded piece of paper by the clerk of the court who had, in turn, been handed the folded piece of paper by Mr Harper, the courthouse security guard, who had been handed it by the placard-waving Miss Winterbottom up in the public gallery.

Judge Humperdink unfolded the piece of paper and read what was written on it. His eyes narrowed and he stared intently at Sunny, who tried to look as small as possible (as though he wanted to disappear).

"Mr Withayew," said the judge squeakily. "Is it true that your name is not, in truth, Mr Withayew but Sunny Grunt and that you are not only not really a lawyer but are also a minor?"

Mrs Grunt let out a snort that would have made Ace and/or Lady Bigg's pig, Poppet, proud. "A miner?" she cackled. "My Sunny a miner? Do you think I'd let him dig underground? He's only a child, you balloon-faced baboon!"

"Silence in—" began the clerk of the court, but Judge Humperdink had had enough and waved his hand for *him* to be silent. "Well?" he demanded, leaning right forward and glaring at poor Sunny.

"Yes," said Sunny. "It's true. My name is Sunny spelled-with-a-'u' Grunt, not Sunny Withayew ... and I'm not a lawyer ... and I *am* a boy."

"Yes!" cried a triumphant lone voice from the gallery. It belonged to Miss Winterbottom, who'd also leaped to her feet and was now waving her placard high above her. (I wonder how she would have felt if she'd known the trouble Sunny went to to pay for her stolen bags of peanuts?) She looked around sheepishly, then sat down again.

Judge Humperdink hadn't taken his eyes off Sunny. The judge looked far from happy. His face was reddening, which made his head look even *more* like a balloon. "I have never in my twenty-five years as a judge been confronted with such a total and disgraceful disregard for the law," he said, his voice getting higher and higher. The real reason for his upset was that having to sort out this Sunny's deception could take ages, and his brown-soup-based luncheon could be seriously delayed!

Sunny was in BIG TROUBLE.

Whereas before Mimi and the others had been filled with wonder at Sack's success in having every charge against Mr Grunt dismissed, they now feared for poor young Sunny.

"Your honour—" began Sack, sounding far less confident this time.

"This had better be good, Mr Sack!" said the judge.

"Sunny Grunt never claimed to be a lawyer. This is my first ever hearing and he is simply assisting me. As for the misunderstanding about his name, he's explained it. He's Sunny with-a-u..."

Mr Benderby was on his feet once more. "Your honour," he said. "Could we please deal with the important charges levelled against Mrs Grunt first and *then* deal with this boy?"

"Very well, Mr Benderby," said Judge Humperdink. "We shall return to the matter of Master Sunny Whatever-Your-Name is later but in the meantime—"

"HUMPTY!" cried out a commanding voice.

The judge shuddered at the name.

Lady "La-La" Bigg'd had enough and was taking matters into her own hands. "Judge Humperdink... You know who I am. I know who I am—"

"Silence in cour—" began the clerk.

"The hearing recognises Lady Bigg," said Judge Humperdink. Then sighed.

"Of course you recognise me, Humpty. I used to talcum powder your bottom when you were a baby."

"I mean, that the hearing officially allows you to be heard."

"This really is most irregular, your honour," said the prosecutor, Mr Benderby.

"Mr Benderby, both of the charges levelled against Mrs Grunt relate to events surrounding the –" The judge consulted a piece of paper. "– Preserves, Jams and Jellies Competition at the country fair. Auntie La-La – I mean Lady Bigg – is not only a member of the country fair committee but was also to have judged this year's Preserves, Jams and Jellies Competition. So it's for that reason that the

hearing officially recognises Auntie La-La –
er – Lady Bigg."

"Thank you, Humpty," said her ladyship.

Mr Benderby sighed and sat down. He was
looking forward to the day being over. It
wasn't shaping up as one of his best.

"I'd just like to say to the court that, as a
committee member and the competition
judge, I speak on behalf of the county fair
when I say that I don't believe any rules were
actually broken by Mrs Grunt," said Lady
Bigg, sounding very posh and formal and
official.

Mr Benderby hauled himself to his feet
again. "And do we have a copy of these rules
anywhere?"

"Yes," said Lady Bigg. She took a piece of
paper out of her pocket, folded it into a paper
plane and threw it from the public gallery.

It did an impressive loop-the-loop that would have made WingCo Fish or Alphonso Tubb proud, and came to a stop, wedged in Judge Humperdink's ear.

"Sorry, Humpty!" laughed Lady Bigg. "I couldn't have done that if I'd tried!"

There was much laughter, including some loud snorts from Ace. This set Poppet off doing some piggy snorts of her own and made Lady Bigg look around.

"Silence in court!" said the clerk of the

court. The judge didn't try to stop him this time.

Judge Humperdink unfolded the paper and smoothed it flat. It said:

COUNTRY FAIR

Rules Regarding Preserves, Jams and

Jellies Competition:

1. The judge's decision is final.

signed

La-La

Lady Bigg

Preserves, Jams and Jellies Competition

Judge

"The judge's decision is final?" he asked.

"Yes," said Lady Bigg.

"That's the only rule?"

"Yes."

"And what is your decision?" asked Judge Humperdink in his unusually squeaky voice.

"That there is no case to answer," said Lady La-La Bigg from the public gallery.

"Then that is my decision too," said the judge, and he would have banged the gavel if he could have done, but all the cheering and clapping made up for the lack of it. When the noise died down, Lady Bigg was still standing.

"As for Sunny, we've all done silly things as children, haven't we, Humpty?"

"Yes, but—" began the judge.

"Embarrassing things we might not want to be mentioned in court?"

"Yes, but—"

"Involving a long car journey and too many cakes—"

"All charges are dropped," said Judge Humperdink, almost shouting. "This hearing is now officially at an end!"

It was soup time at last!

The judge thought of his tie under his official robes. It was yellow! He smiled. Yellow was the perfect background colour for brown-soup-stain islands.

In the courtroom foyer it was congratulations all round. Although Lady Bigg received much praise, the heartiest congratulations went to Sack. He had been a triumph. With all charges dropped there would be no trial, let alone jail, for Mr and Mrs Grunt. They were free to go and not come back. The ex-gardener was the hero of the hour.

Mr Grunt slapped him on the back by way of a thank you then, forgetting why he was hitting him, was about to give him a follow-up kick in the shins. Mrs Grunt stopped him.

"Let me do that!" she said. "Why should you have all the fun?"

Sunny quickly squeezed himself between Sack and his mum.

"How did you come up with all those different laws and acts and stuff?" Sunny asked him. "You were *brilliant*!"

"Thanks," said Sack. "I invented them."

"Invented all those laws?"

"As in made-them-all-up invented them?" asked Mimi in amazement.

"Well, you could put it that way..." said Sack, because it was, of course, true. He'd invented the laws and precedents and acts of parliament he'd quoted in the courthouse

in the same way that he'd invented pens and bikes and shoelaces in the past, and maybe – just maybe – like everything he'd ever invented in the past had turned out to have existed already, it was possible that he'd made up laws that already existed.

Unlikely though, isn't it?

Still, Sack was looking forward to a long career in the Law with a capital L.

Just then, Poppet came squealing past them. She'd lost her straw hat and pushchair but was still wearing lipstick and her floral-patterned dress. Mr Harper, the courthouse security guard, was in hot pursuit.

"No pigs!" he cried. "No pigs!"

The security guard swerved to avoid Mr and Mrs Grunt, who now appeared to be playing a game of marbles – but with glass eyes – between people's legs on the foyer's black-

and-white tiled floor.

Ace wandered over to join Sunny and the others, adjusting the hearing aid behind his ear. "That was cool," he said. "You guys were amazing."

"Thanks for coming," said Sunny. "It really helped to know we had so many people here to support us."

They looked across to Dr Alphonso Tubb and Jenny Prendergast. The pair of them were gazing into each other's eyes as they held hands and whispered to each other.

Sunny, however, was distracted by the appearance of another figure across the lobby floor: a tall, thin woman he'd never met before. But there was something familiar about the way she walked.

"Any idea who that is?" he asked Mimi.

At that moment Mrs Lunge appeared at the woman's side. "Hello, Edna," she said. And hit her across the knees with her enormous handbag before running away. The woman gave chase.

"So that's Edna Tuppenny!" said Sunny. "You know what? I'm willing to bet that *she* was the person spying on us with the binoculars outside Grandma's house. She may have been disguised in a raincoat and cap, but I'd recognise her anywhere, with her sharp shoulders and lollopy walk!"

"I think you're right!" said Mimi excitedly.

"So she was spying on your *grandma* and not you!" said Mimi.

Sunny nodded. "Probably keeping an eye on Grandma's jars of goodies for the competition. But that still doesn't explain who the man was peeping through the window at Green Lawns."

Sunny was interrupted by a tap on the shoulder. He turned round to be confronted by an arm sticking out between two great fronds of leaves. It was Norris Bootle.

"Er, that was me at the window, I'm ashamed to say," said Norris. "I – er – sometimes used to keep an eye on what my rival in love was up to… Not now, of course. Not now that Alphonso and Jenny are officially engaged."

"Then what are you doing here in the courthouse?" asked Mimi. "And why are you hiding behind that big pot plant?"

She had a point, you know.

"Yes. Well … I'm not quite there yet," said Norris, looking lovingly across the foyer to Miss Prendergast. "These things take time." He pulled himself back behind the leaves. "I won't get over the old girl just like that, you know."

They looked back at the loving couple. Even from across the foyer, Ace could read the words "my sweet" and "my little lovey-dove" on Dr Alphonso Tubb's lips. Ace gave another one of his little snorts, the ones that sounded very much like Poppet the pig.

Lady "La-La" Bigg obviously thought so because at that moment she was passing through the foyer in search of her runaway pig, and when she heard the noise it stopped her in her tracks.

She stared Ace in the face.

A strange look passed across her features, like cloud patterns casting shadows on the landscape on a sunny day.

"What... What... What's your name?" she asked. Her voice sounded far less commanding than Sunny'd ever heard it.

"Ace," said Ace.

She gave a little gasp. "Horace?" she said quietly.

It was obvious that the boy had no idea what Lady "La-La" was on about.

But Sunny did.

Was she suggesting...?

Did she mean...?

"Tell her about the blanket," he said.

"The blanket?" said Ace. "Oh, as a baby I was found on the steps of an opera house stage door, Lady Bigg. I was wrapped in a blanket with the word 'ACE' on it, so that's what Lara – the lady who took me in and brought me up – named me."

Lady Bigg couldn't take her eyes off him. She made a noise like a squeak of air escaping from a balloon. "So that's where Biggy must have left you, in your torn blankey!" she said, barely managing to get the words out before bursting into tears.

Ace didn't know what to say or do, so he patted her on the back.

"Horace," she said, pulling herself tightly

against him. "I am your mother."

"My mother?"

"Your mother." She nodded. "For years I've kept the company of pigs because they remind me of your little snorting ways. I've pretended not to care. I've been strong … but I've missed you and your snorting every single day."

Sunny felt a great big lump in his throat (like the time Mrs Grunt had served up golf-ball stew).

Ace didn't know what to think.

"My mother?" he said. "You really are my mother?"

Sunny and Mimi strode towards the exit of

the courthouse. "La-La" Bigg and Ace would probably want time alone together.

Less than an hour later, Ace – or should that be The Honourable Horace Bigg? – and Lady "La-La" Bigg were sitting together in the courthouse car park on the top steps of the Grunts' caravan. She was showing him a photograph. It was of a man with little criss-crosses of sticking plasters on his face and a large parrot on his shoulder: Lord Bigg.

Ace traced the outline of the parrot with a finger.

"The plasters were covering beak-bites," said her ladyship. "The man is your father. The parrot is Monty."

A pirate captain. His dad had a parrot on his shoulder, just like a pirate captain!

"Mother!" he cried, and threw his arms around a very happy "La-La" Bigg.

She wiped away a tear. "That nice Lara Farp will always be your real mum to you, I expect, Horace. And that's OK by me. But it's good to know where you come from, isn't it, and always useful to have a spare... You know, for when your mum is in the wash, or stuck up a tree. My pigsty is your pigsty. Come by whenever you want."

Ace looked at her for a moment, then snorted with delight. Poppet joined in for good measure.

A short distance away, Sunny was feeding Fingers a stale currant bun and a handful of peanuts. He wondered what it must be like to find your birth parents...

He sighed as he gazed up into a nearby tree.

"What are you up to?" demanded Mrs Grunt, who appeared to be brushing her hair with Sharpie, her stuffed hedgehog.

"Oh, nothing," said Sunny. "I was just wondering if that's the same one."

"The same *what*?" demanded Mr Grunt. He was clasping a fistful of thistles. He'd found them growing on the edge of a far corner of the car park and was going to feed them to Clip and Clop.

"The same squirrel," said Sunny, pointing

up into the tree.

Ma Lunge appeared from out of Mrs Grunt's shadow. "Most squirrels hunt in packs," she said. "The other squirrel probably phoned ahead." She sighed.

Mr Grunt was staring at the squirrel, and the squirrel was staring back at Mr Grunt with his big squirrelly eyes. (The squirrel had the squirrelly eyes. Not Mr Grunt.) The squirrel was a rather mangy-looking thing. His tail looked less like fur and more like a large feather that had been used as a quill pen and played with by small, sticky-fingered children.

"That's him all right," said Mr Grunt, and, as if to confirm it, the furry little blighter dashed down the tree trunk and stole one of Fingers'

peanuts from right under the elephant's nose
... well, from under his *trunk*.

Mr Grunt reached up and touched the
dressing and the plaster over his own nose.

"Chrrrrrrrgggggg!" went the squirrel.

Mr Grunt simply grunted.

Uh-oh, thought Sunny. This means *war*.

When my plane got wedged
Upside down in a tree
And I saw my sweet Jenny
Running over to me
A jolly nice thought
Made me think "Yippee!"
That few things are better
Than FAMILY

ALPHONSO TUBB, MD

DOCTOR TO THE STARS

*Read more of the Grunts'
ridiculous antics in:*

THE GRUNTS IN TROUBLE
THE GRUNTS ALL AT SEA
THE GRUNTS ON THE RUN

Search for

nosy crow

on the iTunes App Store for
the free Grunts game for your
iPhone, iPod Touch or iPad,
The Grunts: Beard of Bees

Check out the buzz at
www.meetthegrunts.com